The Sodom an

CW01660704

Also in Arrow Books by Barry N. Malzberg

HEROVIT'S WORLD

Barry N. Malzberg

The Sodom and Gomorrah Business

ARROW BOOKS

Arrow Books Limited
3 Fitzroy Square, London W1

An imprint of the Hutchinson Publishing Group

London Melbourne Sydney Auckland
Wellington Johannesburg and agencies
throughout the world

First published in Great Britain by Arrow Books Ltd 1979
© Barry N. Malzberg 1974

CONDITIONS OF SALE: This book shall not, by way of trade or otherwise, be lent, re-sold, hired out or otherwise circulated without the publisher's prior consent in any form of binding or cover other than that in which it is published and without a similar condition being imposed on the subsequent purchaser. This book is published at a net price and is supplied subject to the Publishers Association Standard Conditions of Sale registered under the Restrictive Trade Practices Act, 1956.

Made and printed in Great Britain
by The Anchor Press Ltd
Tiptree, Essex

ISBN 0 09 914590 1

For Stephanie Jill Malzberg

"God gave me a tail to brush off the flies
but I'd rather have no flies and no tail."

Benjamin the Donkey
(*Animal Farm*, George Orwell)

part one

SODOM AND GOMORRAH

i

Wham! Sitting in the great auditorium of the Institute Death and Disorder One-Oh-Four. Watching the films of those great events of the past, now temporarily stopped, held in perfect crystalline focus. Held. Like artifacts.

The ancient projector whirs into action again, film 16 millimeters in width, 24 frames per second, colors bright, vivid, technochromic. There is old Kennedy again, living for an instant only to die once more.

Junkies on death, all these fucking Kennedys.

The brains are blown clear through the old bugger's skull. A slender rosy halo crowns the crimson explosion. He falls into his wife's arms.

Then the long shapely legs of his wife as she scrambles for the door.

The action stops. The whir and clatter of the second reel begins. Here is Kennedy II, spilling his brains in a filthy, garbage-strewn kitchen (Couldn't they have cleaned it for the event?), the eyes calm, almost serene, curiously untouched by the violence, as though pain of death has absolved him of everything, falling, focused, watching the angles of the camera.

He has great theatrical presence, that Kennedy.

And Watts. Blacks race out of stores, clutching TVs, stereos, radios. Militants with bushy afros, long dashikis, black berets, all clenching fists and shouting slogans.

L.A. erupts into earthquakes, fissures, flames, a fiendish tribute to an age of hell.

Then Chicago in the eighties when the Twin Towers toppled, and the Prudential Building went.

Lawson's knee prods mine. I prod his in return, day-dreaming vaguely of train wrecks, auto collisions, plane crashes—of sexual connection. I ponder taking him down the hall to one of the study cubicals, where we would divest ourselves of our martial uniforms—our epaulets, chevrons, ribbons, medals—to grasp and gasp again, as the film rolls, the fires roar, the guns crash, the dance goes on.

Now Wallace has seized his stomach in the shopping center and the violence rolls on, on, on—King, Evers, Chappaquiddick, Malcolm X—till the reel spins to a stop, the tag end flapping against the machine, flickering its flopping, ticking shadow on the screen.

The lights go on.

Lawson and I, we blink, our eyes blinded by the little stabs of light that come from the ceiling like candles. Through the loudspeakers the lecture begins. Every time you see something interesting in the films they hammer you with lectures. This is the price we pay for knowledge. It is a price we pay, knowing that the duller the lectures the more interesting have been the clips.

"The common denominator," the lecturer says, "we must seek the common denominator in all of the events we have just seen recalled. So consider, ponder some of this if you will. What have you seen here? What is the underlay? Where the link?"

Lawson and I wink at one another. We touch hands in the pause; moderate excitation, slow tumescence. "All of this," the lecturer says, "occurred in the cities.

"Occurred in the cities," the voice continues. "Urbanopolis, agglomeration, cultural flux and flow. Lag, crime, disease, tension, murder, incursion against the extant systems. Consider!" he adds ecstatically, "all of this known again in the great population centers which in the middle part of the century became the primary life situation for eighty percent of the culture. Do you follow all of this so far?"

The lecturer died many years ago. What we are seeing is a plasticized, life-size reproduction of the lecturer programmed with speech. It is an old process, originated in the 1960's I do believe, but only reconstituted within the past five years at the Institute to save expenses, and a most remarkable process it is. Although the mannequin is waxen, the devices are extremely realistic, and it is hard to realize that he would topple if the podium was suddenly rushed and pressure exerted against the form. Some errant students are rumored to have done this a year or years ago; they were instantly expelled. So desire will rumble along at the mere level of expectation.

"Think of the solution," the speaker is saying, "the solution! It was staring authorities in their collective faces. The problems were obvious: rising alienation, violence, other factors cited all happening in direct correlation to the incidence of urban centers. The compression of population, too many thrust into little space, congestion, breakdown, failure of the geometrics of space." The mechanized lecturer is babbling incoherently but the machinery often breaks down. "Check all of your references on this tomorrow. Research! Government seeking and finding the solution at last was initially hesitant to seize procedures as bureaucratic processes force delimitation of reality for accommodation. Then throughout the period of burning hastened themselves along that course so briefly ordained, now accelerating, *always* accelerating."

Film again. Now the Network is seen from a great height: a mile or more straight up, mingling in the clouds, the outlines of our buildings and roads and people vaguely perceived. Jagged those outlines; they stick out like sickly chancres through the overcast. Network is a piss-poor place; we do not have to be shown that.

Oh, richly, richly does Death and Disorder deserve its wretched reputation. Not thirty minutes into this first class of the initial session the plastic lecturer stumbles in reverse, arms flailing, legs running amuck, gears grinding. He says: "Orientation is now concluded. Reading lists distributed in the corridors." And the lights go on full, revealing students and the hall.

ii

A tiny, mad animal of an idea starts to flutter within, touching its tiny claws to the purpose. I can see the degeneration of the Institute—not unlike that of the ancient cities before it—and no less I sense my own deterioration. There must be a way to spite the Institute and to bring some excitement to our lives, and we will find it or this is not the Institute.

Remarkable! I am already thinking like a denizen of the cities. Activity is all that matters.

iii

I propose my idea to Lawson during mess. "Yes," he says, his little eyes narrowing, "yes, yes indeed, but there is much to be done, is there not?"

He puts down a fork, his military sleeve insignia bobbing with the motion, and says, "We'll need a car."

"That's easy."

"How easy?"

"They have a pool, of course."

"And we'll need to cover the time," Lawson says. "Time is the essence."

"Seniors are exempted."

"That still means the barriers. We're going to have to cross the barriers."

"That will be easy, too," I say. "All obstacles are ash once one has found purpose. This is one of the lessons of decision. We are soldiers, guardians, protectors. We have privileges."

"And of course we'll need weapons."

"I'll take care of that," I say. "Let me make those arrangements too."

I know that I have touched him. Life in the Institute is pleasant and dull, contained and simple, it gives us an authoritarian environment, an authoritarian set of principles: how to live, when to sleep, how to eat, drink, drug, emit. Who needs this shit, in short.

"In only months," I point out to Lawson later, "we will be soldiers and have patrol responsibilities of our own. Aren't we entitled then to see the terrain, to understand those elements for which we are being conditioned? This is the rationale which truly impels. I know that we can live with this."

He nods his approval.

iv

From the abandoned armory, one bored part-time guard there, I find a wonderful old 1964 Cadillac in running condition. Power windows, power seats, climate control, none of them working. Four hundred and twenty-eight cubic inches in the overhead valve V-8, a wonderful, brown stain spreading from rear-quarter panels through to the fender skirts, both of which, interestingly, are intact. The engine produces flame only with the slightest urging; I manage to set timing from ancient manuals. The attendant looks at me with interest; he is not exactly sure of the limits of his duties. Does he stop me or not? He does not; he is an underclassman and the intensity of my purpose discourages him. We talk a little about the old internal-combustion machine, a device which I regard with as much reverence as my ancestors. Nothing will truly replace it in my desires; the device *works*. Cadillacs were among the most expensive of domestic automobiles and even with this diseased artifact there is a feeling of pervasive quality, although again it may only be my own sense of excitement. The radio in the car still works and I listen to status reports to cheer me on my work.

Lawson meanwhile is working himself. He, in fact, produces one antique pistol, five beautiful hand grenades, two handfuls of poison capsules, in addition to the usual elevators. The poison is in case of capture, of course.

"We will protect the integrity of the Institute," he says. His influence appears to be ancient films, whereas mine is founded upon texts. Each to his own, of course, although I find him irritating.

"Don't be ridiculous," I say with a little tickle of fear. "We're perfectly safe, armed as we are."

"Maybe not so. You never know. They are malevolent and dangerous."

"We'll be safe," I insist, "perfectly safe. Also, they're wary of outsiders, let alone two outsiders from the Institute. We'll be identifiable through our military insignias."

"Not necessarily"

"They only kill one another."

"So we have been told."

"It's true!" I say, "it's true!" thinking of the pistons and levers in the Cadillac, pure machinery, the glint of that recollected steel comforting me, although I find myself shouting with a sudden burst of fear, "There's nothing hazardous to it at all!"

"Don't be sure," Lawson says, looking grim, flipping me two of the poison capsules. They bounce off my chest like little balls, and I must scramble to retricvc them, one by one, from the floor. Awful consequences if they are discovered on room check; surprise checks are frequent in military school. "I know only," he adds, "that they want us to believe certain things. But there is a great difference between that which they would have us accept and the objective truth of the matter."

"Not necessarily."

"Otherwise," he says, "why go at all? If it is just as they tell us then there is no need to do field research, is there? Perhaps," he says cunningly, "you've changed your mind on this expedition then."

"No. Never."

"Are you quite sure?"

"I want to go. It was my idea," I say. "You have to remember that."

"They may seize your brain, destroy your mind, change your impulses."

"I'm not a child."

"They are cunning and vicious," he points out. "They often attack from the rear. They are very hostile toward the Institute."

"Ridiculous," I say. I should point out our position

in more detail at this time, objectify as it were the rigid parameters of this discussion, fill in physical detail, background, interweave expository sections with the intensity of dialogue, but I will not. There is no quality of background to my life; all is foreground: intensity, clutching. Originally I had hoped not to go to the Institute, to seek something more artistic for myself, but people of our social class are lucky to find any kind of career and the Institute was inevitable. Actually, I am not at all authoritarian.

"They shall pass upon us the various and terrible oaths of their tribes. Then they will torture us secretly in the practices of cults which are not even known to the Institute personnel."

His eyes are savage. Always in our special relationship that savagery has been there, sado-masochism, the perfect ambivalence of purposes. I decide that sooner or later I will have to give this serious thought. Graduation will separate us; he will assume his post, I mine. We will be broken and that will be the end of that. Different checkpoints, different locales and, eventually, granted the full privileges of staff, I will be able to find females and perhaps even marry. They do not subject us indefinitely to this kind of existence; I have met senior personnel and heard their stories.

"Nothing will happen," I say again, knowing that he is baiting me. "You know that as well as I do. So don't try to stop me."

"There are roving bands. They can overturn cars, torch them, smash up the windshields. They can demand," he avers, hovering over me, "they can demand our complete sexual surrender."

His mouth breaks open in a toothly canine sneer.

v

We are reminded in class the next day of the mysterious coincidences and circumstances that surrounded the assassination of John F. Kennedy. The strange murder of the accused assassin; the hurried efforts of secret-service personnel to close the coffin; the hasty and insufficient inquest; the departure of the opposing party leader hastily from town the morning of the assassination; the peculiar deaths of fifteen to twenty people who claimed special knowledge of the assassination within a period of only a few months . . . oh, it is complex and interesting material and the lecturer, a different one (coils, tapes, and wires raggedly exposed, poor quality control), bids that we pay this the most serious attention as Zapruder, our conduit, is run over and over again on the huge wall facing us.

"You must remember," the lecturer says, "that the crime has never been entirely solved"—he ambulates to the front of the stage, waves a little plastic forefinger—"although," he concedes, "it is perfectly true that much of history is beyond recollection, beyond order, and the normal state of our affairs is to exist completely cut off from our history, seeing it only as in poorly shaped dreams. Nevertheless," he says, returning to the subject, "it was a purely urban disaster in the sense that the assassination of one earlier president may be considered to be rural; congestion, dislocation are purely urban phenomena and this must be taken into account." Briefly we see a flick of the third Kennedy on the stones. "People became certain during the nineteen-sixties," he says, "that they had to leave the cities. By the nineteen-eighties implementation was complete and what were left in the cities were no longer people. Which did not in the main," he concludes, "make life any easier, of course."

vi

So Lawson and I, we take our passes and we go into the Network. The car, waiting by the armory for us, hubcaps painstakingly replaced and antenna ripped off (no unnecessary protrusions at any time), starts easily; it snaffles at the road like a dog sniffing game as we leave the Institute far behind us. It dangles its little mufflers like dugs; the air-conditioning system without freon fails to work; there is a bad miss at low rpm—but then that remarkable car, the Cadillac, remembers its heritage and settles into a droning, steady forty, propelling us toward the jagged skyline at the New York ruins. I drive with perfect concentration, feeling union with the machine, its own quality pouring through my fingertips and arms. An extraordinary thing to be driving in such control and quiet.

Lawson, he sits at an uneasy distance. He has brought along vials and pops ups and downs, while I, driver by demand, apply myself to the power brakes, the variable-ratio power-steering, the foot-formed accelerator, half-recollected pages of exposition from the owner's manual and old films opening themselves up to me as I ease the car through the ancient pot-holed roads, the headlights scanning the road like a lighthouse beacon probing the surface of a dark and brooding sea.

A fit limousine for our expedition into the N.Y.C.

We are alone, quite alone, twelve miles of road from the Institute to barrier, time enough to think of turning back but we do not. I wait for Lawson to suggest that we give up the expedition and he waits for me to do the same and neither of us do it at all. The car, guiding us, continues. Never has the Institute struck me with as much sentimental force as' it does now—the bright, aseptic corridors; the nightsticks carried by the supervisors; the glorious music which fills the halls throughout the evening, the martial airs and old war chants!—but one cannot remain rooted in time. Life is an ongoing process, or so I remind myself.

"Life is an ongoing process," I say to Lawson, who does not reply. In most ways he is my intellectual inferior. It is my fault that we became so linked, but actually, I was lazy. Pair-bonding is the path of least resistance.

At the gate a guard, youthful and with grief-stricken eyes, holds up a hand to retain us, looking exactly like an ancient poster of the type which must have so engaged me. To be stopped is unusual. We know from our informal knowledge of the procedures of Network that the checkpoints are not applied seriously nowadays. There is so little traffic, after all, into the Network. The policy seems to be that anyone who wants to go into that place will deserve what he gets there . . . but then again, every time policy seems predictable it reverses, proving that rambles in the dormitories, procedures in the Institute, are incomplete conditioning. It would seem. Not to speculate. One never knows. Perhaps.

Lawson spreads against the door as we stop. He puts up feet on the upholstery, demonstrating the distance between the two of us to the guard by making slow circles with his palm. Already he is trying to give the impression that he is a passenger, that this is my expedition—or then again he may be seeking to deny the more specifically sexual content of our relationship. (Homosex is accepted; I do not want to give the impression that it is not. The Institute itself approves of homosex and has formalized the pair-bondings, but one is not to say how deeply official policy has been formulated to strangers . . . better then to be circumspect.)

"Going in?" the guard asks. I nod. "You'd better forget about it," he says. His line of sight is nervous and rather transfixed; he looks beyond us, piecing out the sky. "They're having the wars down there tonight. Clear, clean reports."

Despite the fact that he bears a carbine, the guard seems inept. He should be; barrier duty is the lowest of all specialties for which Institute training is appropriate, even lower than urban sweep, which as we know is a job for the brainless. Urban sweep, however, involves a certain necessary proficiency with incendiaries and also a control of the normal fear of heights, whereas barrier duty is a job for the inarticulate, the moodless, the narcoticized, if you will . . . men upon whom the landscape, solitude, and boredom will have no effect at all. The guard stinks of cheap scent; it is hard to believe but quite likely that he is an alcoholic.

"Down on Southway, that is," the guard is saying. He brings gun to heart, suggestively. "They're killing each other on the avenues. It's no place for boys."

"Maybe," Lawson says, taking no offensive, the downers afflicting him with massive calm, "but it's no problem for us. We can handle Southway." I understand once again why I feel his worth so deeply, why the pair-bond was inaugurated. He can control situations in a way that I cannot; he has a certain confidence and flair, whether drug-induced or merely exacerbated I am not in a position to say. "We'll skirt Southway altogether. We've got other plans for our time in there."

"Westerly's not so fucking good either," the guard says. Thoughts of Westerly make his voice flat, his features dull. "None of it is any fucking good. Those animals in there are on the prowl."

"Don't shit us," Lawson says and passes the guard a downer. "We're going in."

I throw the car into neutral (it is overheating, the red light says) and race the engine. "Fuck the travelogue," Lawson says, "fuck your reports. We are going in. Access to Network," he says then, quoting the codes, "cannot be denied any citizen with proper credentials."

The guard nods. "That's true," he says. "I didn't say you couldn't go in. I just said—"

"The purpose of the barriers, you fool, is to keep the inmates *out,"* Lawson says and slams me in the ribs, indicating that I am to shift the car into drive and begin. It is a good suggestion, it would be a proper point of termination, but something has happened to the gears and the car is locked in neutral. I work at the shift lever, back and forth; the car buckles down into drive finally and stalls. Shit. Laboring, I work to restart it.

"Screw it," the guard is saying meanwhile, inattentive to my struggles. He shrugs. "Institute," he grumbles. "Institute fellows. Right?"

"That's us," Lawson says. "Pride of the Institute. Death and Disorder One-Oh-Four."

"That makes the situation a little different then, doesn't it?"

"Yes," Lawson says, "it changes everything." He sits more alertly, drawing his knees together.

The car, revived, stalls. Low rpm's will do it to the overhead valve V-8 every time, although this knowledge is no comfort. Swearing, I try once again to start the Cadillac. Lawson looks at me without affection. "Get it going," he says.

"I'm trying."

"I don't really give a damn who you fuckers are," the guard says. "I was just going through questioning because they make us do that. Actually, I don't give a shit. I don't give a shit about any of you."

"Good," Lawson says. The starter clicks, failed solenoid somewhere in the bowels of the car. There is something seriously wrong with the mechanism, but this is something that should have been attended to back in the armory. No time to worry about it now, although there is a clear premonition of difficulty. At the fifth try I am finally able to mesh gearing. The car pants.

"You've got your warnings," the guard says. "I've done

everything I'm supposed to do with you. It's up to you now."

"We intend."

"Observation troops, you said?"

"Something like that," Lawson says. The car enlarges with the shots of fuel I am laying in through the accelerator. "Get going," he says.

"Undercover troops," the guard says slyly, peering into the car. "That's what you must be, right? Checking out the terrain."

"Exactly," I say. At last the car is running, although missing badly. I drop into drive and for a moment there is a feeling that it will stall once again, then it gathers power. I creep it forward.

"Time we had some observation in there," the guard says. "Maybe you're reconaissance, huh? Check them out, then move in with the heavy stuff. Goddamned place," his voice is beginning to fade as the car has now opened up a full length on the barrier, "this place is going to blow we don't get some sense out of it. Well, then. Anyway. How are things at the dear old place these days, not that I miss the hole."

"Pleasant and dull," Lawson says, turning, leaning out the window because we are now down the road a bit. "Just the way it was always." He gives me a sign. I threw the accelerator into the floorboards. There is a crumbling sound and then the engine roars. The car begins to move rapidly.

We are on a long, dead road, the barrier and post already diminished to rear-view. The guard waves at us, taking on a rather plaintive aspect from this distance. I glance at the little figure in the rear-view mirror, adjusting it, then give full attention to the road.

"Southway, Northing, Westerly, Easto, fuck them all," Lawson says, "fuck them *all,* we'll blow them up, you hear me?"

It seems to be a rather overoptimistic portrayal of the true role of Institute personnel in regard to the environment, but then again I can understand his elevation, can in fact even share it.

"Fuck them all!" he shrieks and the Cadillac rolls; we stream across the dense, dull waters of the Hudson River and touch the Network itself. It is quite an awesome feeling to be there at last, although, of course, there is no difference in the immediate terrain. It merely seems to compact around us as we move south.

Lawson, he breaks out another of the uppers and ingests one, a strange, ashen look of solemnity spreading across his face.

vii

It occurs to me, driving, that if necessary, if pushed to defiance, I would have killed the guard. Why not? He would hardly be missed and barrier maintenance is an assignment of such low repute that there is not even a back-up or alternating shift; the guard himself is responsible for the post. When he sleeps the post is closed down, and so on. It would have been very easy to kill him.

Violence begins at home, I understand; to enter upon the Network is to take upon oneself the obligation of ancestors who would have killed the guard without a thought, not out of hatred but simply because it had to be done. All right. All right, it would have come out of hatred as well, but that would have been the less important factor; reluctance, necessity would have guided the gun closing in upon me. He would have opened under the spent bullet like a flower, falling, bleeding in spent little petals down his pitiable and earth-stained uniform.

It is difficult, difficult to apprehend what I have become but then, on the other hand, better now than later, I think; and as I think so I help myself to one upper, driving one-handed, the car rocketing as smoothly as some primeval beast into the center of our history. *Wham!*

viii

Northing, we know, is the most dangerous of all. Here the bands have the advantages of terrain. Tacked to the mainland, it contains hundreds of secret passages to the landscape, all of which must be covered by the barriers . . . but new access is being found constantly by the bands, and thus Northing is the bloodiest of them all. Most of the great sweeps have occurred there. The bands scoot, laying down their direction in little fibers of what I see as energy; now and then they come straight upstate to be found wandering, seeking death, and the sweepers come in then to clean out the area. If there is ever a true infiltration of our land, then, it will come from Northing and its advantages.

Still, still: Northing has open space and patches of land which arc toward the fields upstate, natural advantages of terrain not given to, say, Southway, which is not even a pretty place. For that reason, at least based upon the materials I have studied (firsthand knowledge of any part of the Network in the Institute's opinion is too dangerous to attempt), I think that I am fonder of Northing than of the other sections. Perhaps. Also Northing is an undeclared area; it is open to all of the bands, unlike Westerly and Easto, which are formally at war and hence ripped by maneuvers at all times, demanding almost constant sweep to keep the bands in place. A man could asphyxiate in Easto and Westerly sometimes. Southway, which we understand to be rioting tonight, is the only section, oddly enough, without distinct identity. It borrows Northing's landscape, the meanness of Easto, the murk of Westerly . . . but fails to add any distinct quality of its own. Too bad for the inhabitants, but then, they are not elevated types. Lacking some natural advantages, these bands have to make it on malevolence.

Into Northing then. Northing is difficult enough for two fresh-faced little seniors from the Institute, making their initial reconnaissance toward Network. Hostility, yes . . . but a proper humility must overtake even if it is only induced by fear.

"Look," Lawson says as the car rolls, raises his hand, points. "Look at that now."

I look. We are moving through a dense, gutted area; the high smell of the air, darkness in all but that which spills from the headlights guided by autotronic eye. Initially I do not see what he is suggesting—but then, following Lawson's point, I see the activity:

Forms scuttle, whisks of shape, the sound of crackling. The bands are moving tonight. Or perhaps it is only a solitary in the trees having a look at a strange car. Automobiles do not come often to this place and the husks left in the Network are almost all inoperative. Cutoff of fuel supplies.

"Let's take them," Lawson says, touching me roughly, forcing me to slow. "Come on, that's what we're here for, isn't it?"

"Now? Right now?"

"Why not?" He looks at me sidelong. "Did you think we were here for anything else?"

"We don't even know who they are," I say, riding the power brake. The car twitches to a stop. "Shouldn't we at least know—"

"More's the fun. If they were personnel they'd identify themselves, you know. Are you afraid?"

"No," I say quickly. "I'm not afraid. Did you think I came here for that?"

"I don't know," he says. "Let's not talk about it. Let's go. Let's take them."

"I'm not afraid," I say again. The point is obscurely important, at least to me. "Not at all."

"So let's go," he says, "let's go."

I know his lust. I have dreamt it myself in a thousand corridors, embraced those desires I can barely understand. I hear Lawson's rasp. His breath rales against the partitions of esophagus and I am touched by this.

"They're coming closer," he says. "I can sense those things."

Truly, at this moment he sounds like me. If the pills have brought me down they have sent Lawson up and out. He is excited. Excited and happy. This then is what brought him into the Network. It is a difficult insight, that my partner came here to murder.

Not so me. I can live with his desire but I did not come here to murder. I had more complex reasons. "Maybe we should move," I say cautiously. I feel for the first time leached to this doomed Cadillac. It is one thing at the Institute to plan the trip and build the car, assemble the incendiaries. To siphon gasoline, banter with guards, and think of murder. It is quite another, though, to be at darkening rest on a street in Northing waiting for something, *something* to close in upon us. I am not ashamed of this fear, although I am surprised.

"Let's make a reconnaissance sweep," I say, trying to sound professional. "That would be the best. To see the territory. We can always return."

"Bullshit."

"What?"

"Bullshit," he says again. The old word sounds harsh, it shatters. He works out another tab, puts it patiently into his mouth, takes it down. "Stop quivering. You disgrace us. You disgrace the Institute."

"I'm not. I'm not quivering." I place my open hand on the wheel, look down. It is as he says. Indeed, I am quivering, but it is an impersonal fear; it hits to a basic level that I do not understand.

"Yes you are," he says. He moves on the seat; his face is quite remote. "This is no time for delay."

"Yes it is. It's the best time for delay; I can't think of a better one."

"Is it?" he says. "It is? This is what we wanted, remember. Say it! Know it! Know what sent us in here. Move the probe, faggot."

The ancient impulse makes me shake; I know that he is right. Lawson is always right. He takes yet another upper (I am worried about his metabolism now; how much can even he tolerate?), meditates, considers, all in a trice while the sounds leap upon us. "We'll get the bastards," he says. "We'll get the bastards."

"All right," I say. I cannot tolerate this anymore. "We'll get the bastards but I'm not a faggot. I'm not, that has nothing to do with it, I—"

"All right."

"I said *I'm not a faggot,"* I say, my voice rising, I must confess with some difficulty, toward a shriek; I do not really want to lose control in this way, but the charge is central, it has much to do with the context of my life, and if it is to be believed I would have to centrally alter certain assumptions which I will not. I will not. *"I'm not—"*

"All right," he says, "all right, enough." He points. I follow the angle of his finger and I realize that the discussion, however vital, must be terminated.

There are forms around the car.

Two of them, possibly there are three: a man, a woman, something indeterminate lurking behind. Probably their cover. I see those faces as they close on me and yes, yes, they are the faces of Network as I have always known them to be, my first direct experience and a confirmation of all the tapes, for there they are indeed: implacable, rooted, ageless, prints in the Zapruder flex. *They are not what we are, they are entirely foreign,* we cannot understand them no matter how we try and yet, if nothing else, the Institute has made this clear to us: We must understand them or we must die. We will have to be quick and clever in shooting out their bodies from underneath them or otherwise we will be conquered.

Lawson rolls down his window. Caught by the motion the forms circle to that side, the largest one, the man, leading. But we have been cunning, the motion is to lead them over; unleashing my own pistol now I level it down upon them, seeing that the third, the one I had thought to be their cover, is merely the smallest and slowest of the three. Possibly it is a child, then—they still hold to the principle of the nuclear family—which scuttles dependently behind. Lawson gives me a wink and then leans out the window. At this time I have my pistol leveled. Confidence is utterly within me and I know that I can kill when the time has come. All indecision has vanished. Murder is the purpose for which I was created.

Leaning out the window, Lawson has said nothing. There is nothing he needs to say. All that we have to do is wait. Therefore, he waits.

"Please," the man says finally. He talks a distinct English, as flat and unaccented as our own. Transfer of language is easy; even the barbarians can speak clearly. "Please," he says again.

"Please what?" Lawson says. "What do you want from us?" He giggles to himself, seeing the flash of my pistol leveled over his shoulder. I know what he means.

"You're from the outside, aren't you?"

"Are we?"

"Of course you are," the man says. I can see him rather more distinctly now as my eyes come to focus. He is a short, disheveled creature who wears the rags of the Network, yet who—and this is shocking—has the general appearance and motions of one of our instructional kits. Is it possible that they, too, are mannequins? It is certainly fascinating in conception, that both Institute and Network are occupied by dead forms, transacting perverse visions through layers of time and space, but I instantly reject this as untenable. It could not be. Nothing could be this mad; the Institute is real and the Network is real and somewhere between that collision it is necessary for us to survive. The man seems to be about fifty, although they age rapidly out here; probably he is no older than I. "I know that you're from the outside," he is saying. "You have to be. There are grass stains on the wheels," he says, pointing almost shyly toward the hubcaps. "That's how I could tell."

"All right," Lawson says, "this is true. We are from the outside." He seems to be taken by the villain's cleverness, although I had already suspected that these people could think. "We come from the outside." He ingests yet another tab. Truly, I am beginning to become worried about him, and yet how is he to stop? I would not consider smashing the uppers from his hand, which now skirts the jacket, making sure that the packet is safe. He smiles at my gun and then takes out his own, fondles it. Steady now, steady.

"Steady," I say to him. The woman is not clearly in my line of sight and yet it is she who I want to locate. The man looms before my gun, filling it, the woman having fallen away.

"I'm steady," Lawson says, "do you think I'm not? Who are you?" he says to the man before I can answer. "What are your plans? Describe your background, please. What is your view of life in the city? What do you think of what the city has become? Please answer our questions quickly and to the point. We are a field-research team and we are here to try and help you. The more that we can learn, the better your life can become."

"Please," the man says again. He is impermeable, the nuances of rhetoric evade him, as well they might. Now, closer to us, his face is no longer aged and prematurely withered as I had thought, but has instead become that of a child overtaken by pain. Network is a difficult place; let us understand this and no misgivings. Would Lawson or I look any better after years here? "You've got to get us out of this. Northing."

"Yes," the woman says, moving beside him. She touches

his arm. I look at her, trying to form some impression in my mind which will enable me to determine once and for all whether I truly desire females and would be capable with them, but it is hard in this darkness to see anything. Her touch on the man's arm infuriates me; she has no right to do this here. It is merely a taunt. "We've been waiting for seasons for someone to come," she is saying. "This has got to be a sign."

(Low superstition, popular among the cults and bands of the Network. The belief in rampant determinism for all, of course, except oneself, who is likely to be saved by miracles and magic. Lecturers have gone into all of these details. I am sure that I could function with her if truly forced to do so; if worse came to worse I could perform buggery and make believe that it was Lawson. This faith inflames me with new confidence, although it may be simply an extension of my panic. What if I were unable to function with a woman? It would make all of my previous and hard-bought assumptions out to be lies.)

Meanwhile, saying this, she backs from the side of the car. Entreaty is the only confidence that she has had to give. Instead, she has moved from Lawson, comes toward my own open window. Panicking, I try to close it but the damned mechanism jams and I am left hanging stupidly in the car, my melon of a face peering out the window toward the woman's. She is younger than the man, although then again she may be older; the point is that she seems to be less afflicted by the diseases of the Network. In a parody of tenderness I find my hand reaching toward her cheekbones, grotesquely I stroke those high ridges, finding that they feel little differently from the flesh of my own face. There is nothing alien about them; they are merely ourselves in softer masks. She permits my stroke, her eyes looking past me in some absent way, through the car, past Lawson's face and into the eyes of the man who is on the other side. Her eyes flicker with sudden knowledge, I see them take on purpose. She believes that she has moved me.

Abruptly I know that I will kill.

I have suppressed this knowledge to this point; it was, after all, so highly generalized, but now it has hardened to focus; I have found the necessary objects. I will kill these individuals. I file that thought away since it will not affect what will happen for the next few moments, merely knowing that it is still there, locked to the interior like some bauble which can at any time be tapped to give off its explosion of light. As I think of all this my hand falls from her cheek and comes to my own; I feel the stain of her spreading through me at this transference of touch. Lawson giggles.

"We can hide in the trunk," she says. My touch has not affected her; that translucency of face might have been cold glass for all the difference it has made. "Just get us past the barriers and we'll take leave of you." Her voice is strong, flat, conventionalized, but somehow vaguely exciting. "You must get us into the barrier."

The man nods at this, having taken a widened stance. "That's all," he says, "that is all we want."

"Let you into the car?" I say. "We can't possibly have you in the car." Thinking of this I cut off the motor, a daring act. Fast restarts on a hot motor are difficult with these ancient solenoids. Now, surely, we are locked to confrontation with these people; there is no rapid exit. I hold the gun steady. I am excited.

"You came to tour the Network," the man says, talking to Lawson, poking an elbow against Lawson's half-open window. "Now and then there are people like you who come to see. Who want to know how to live, to undig the system. Take us with you out there and we can give you much information."

"Can you?" I say. "What information can you give?" Lawson's breath goes *whoop!* in the darkness. I ram a knee against his, not only for quiet but to reestablish connection. The scene is tense. It is a very tense scene. Little background flickers of light, dim sounds to the east indicate activity. The man looks back that way and then into the car. "We need a great deal of information."

"We can tell you," the woman says, "we know all the secrets of what you call the Network. We're peaceable citizens, sir, it's the others who are in the bands. All we want to do is live our lives, take out the period of exile, return to the land. We have no desire to attack."

"Haven't you?"

"No. We can give you full details of plans in Easto, separate bands, aggressive forces who plan to do something violent to the land. Risking all, we will tell you what they intend; all that we ask in favor is that you take us out of here."

They must have planned all of this carefully. It has a rehearsed quality which does not, of course, make it any less entertaining; rarely have I been made to feel as important as I do at this moment. "You've got to do this," the woman says.

Simple ragged clothing parts and then I believe that I can see her breast, something round and full coming from a parting of clothing. It is so dark; it is difficult to tell. The thing that is a child mews behind her. She darts away, casts a quick, stricken glance toward the ground, then fixes upon me again. Torn between the desire to seize the child and to entrance me, the confusion is clear. I can sympathize with her problem, applaud her decision when it comes. She remains locked to me. The mews continue. "You must," she says.

I take out my gun fully then. Before this it has dangled from a hand, dangled into a fold of jacket. Now I expose it to her as if I had whisked a tumescent prick out of clothing to give her a look at the real treasures. Indeed, my erection is throbbing below, painfully full of conviction, urging me onward. It is disgraceful that I should be excited at a time as crucial as this, but on the other hand my problems must be considered. "Do you see this?" I say to her.

"Yes. I see it."

"This is an antique Smith and Wesson point thirty-two caliber pistol. It is a poor weapon for population control but in close quarters has been found to be most effective. Furthermore, it is in perfect condition."

She nods slowly. Her mouth parts; she looks as if she might take the pistol between her lips. An old obscene image, half-buried through layers of recollection, suddenly reasserts itself and I feel my erection literally tumbling from my clothing.

"Get back," I say.

Lawson has taken out his own gun. On the opposite side, he points it at the man. We must present a terrifying picture to them, the two of us with our pistols, aiming as if to render judgement upon them. Which we are. What is going on? they must be thinking. The man back pedals slowly from the window. His mouth is clenched.

"No," he says, "this is impossible. I've reckoned of it but it is not to be." He is full of conversation, whereas the woman is a more sensible type. She merely attends, unmoving. "I don't believe it," he says.

But he does believe it. He has always believed, I can see this now; the sinful and dreadful violence of their lives has accustomed them well to the leaving of them. This is one of the platitudes of the Institute, as I recollect it having been delivered by the lecturers. Certainly it will hold well in this instance.

"Nothing's impossible," Lawson says. He is totally fixed upon the man as I am upon the woman, but the woman is quiet, she hovers, by the window, she says nothing. "Not in the Network, you fool, don't you know that? Haven't you studied the landscape here? Don't you know where your lives are taking place? And don't you know what this is?"

The man nods once slowly, glumly. "Yes," he says then, "yes, I know what it is. This is a free-fire zone."

Lawson smiles.

He pulls the trigger and the weapon fires.

Meaning, the man falls from us. There is a wet sound

as he hits the turf of Northing and then those moans cease. The woman, she tries to dive through the window, her hand outstretched for my gun, but geometrics do not permit this sort of thing. She smashes her forehead against the implacable panels of the Cadillac . . . and she falls.

Lawson giggles again. He motions down to the vacant space by the window where the man had been. "My first kill," he says. I nod in approbation. He peers from the window, grimaces as if his neck is sprung, then comes back into the car. "Look," he says. "I did it."

"I know you did it."

"I wanted to do it," he says, "I always wanted to do it," and then he begins to sweat, all of the pores of his body open like meteor impacts and from each of them comes a clear stream of water, almost as if he were coming from all of these crevices. He submits to the imposition gracefully, grins, falls back upon the seat then, squeezed out. His eyes close. He seems to be embarked upon the sweetest and saddest of the post-coital sleeps. I let him do this. None of it is any longer my concern.

Instead, I look at the woman.

Slowly she has regained precarious balance, is clutching onto the ledge of the open window like a mountain climber. Her face looms at me harsh and unyielding, yet at the center of those eyes is a maddened wink of comprehension, as if she were about to impart some enormous and central secret.

"You're crazy," she says.

"Oh yes, indeed," I say. I do not really see how I could quibble with this important point. "That happens to be true."

"You've got to be. To do a thing like that." She reaches into the window, grip restored. "You must think we're not human," she says.

"To the contrary," I say, "to the contrary, I think you're completely human. Let me prove this to you. Let me prove my estimate of your humanity," and so I pass my pistol over to the rather astonished Lawson, lurch from the car, managing to topple her in the opening action of the door, and drag her over to a little clump of bushes where I set upon her like sainted Zapruder himself, and to prove my estimate of her humanity, my worth, my dismal need, I rape the shit out of her. The childish form, toddling over into the shadows, watches this gloomily. Surely I would do the same. It is a difficult thing to observe a parent being raped, although I have never, truly speaking, had parents and thus am not able to talk forcefully to this point.

ix

About the act itself possibly the less that is said the better. Pure scatology, pure sexual description and reminiscence was outlawed by the ancient and remarkable statutes after the brief period of permissiveness of the nineteen-sixties and I do not wish to sully this essentially narrow and modest memoir in a way which would offend those who might be privileged to share it with me. Sufficient to say that, garments parted, I find her body as familiar as my own (just as I should have known from that deadly whisk of cheek), that there is no mystery in her crevices, strangeness in her moistness, that entering her is very much like entering myself (curved palm grasping the arrow of self) or Lawson but the fact that it is a female fills me with enormous satisfaction because it proves to me what I have always known: that I am capable of functioning with them as easily as any other way. Two or three brief rutting pumps in the underbrush, two groans and snaffles exchanged head to head, her mouth tearing at mine, my teeth ripping away at her little lips and I am already climaxed, spilling into her in little scurryings of the flesh, conveying a part of me to herself and no thanks necessary for this folks, I would hardly expect her to express gratitude for the act although on the other hand there is no reason why she should have found it objectionable nor do I believe she should. Of course the fact that her mate lay dead in the turf, that her child was at some point of distance observing this, that Lawson was twirling and twirling the pistol to obtain good set . . . this might have understandably undercut the true range and incision of her response . . . but I choose to believe that she did not in any basic sense object to what was going on there. Why should she have?

I fell from her like leaves.

Slowly, groaning, feeling as if I were imprinted into that dread ground, I heaved to my navel, knees, groin, came upright then to note her still lying in the gravel, her body jammed to the stones, a faint aura surrounding this, although that halo might only have existed in my rather fevered and disordered consciousness, and then I went back toward the car, hand extended, put that hand into the window and motioned for Lawson to hand me my pistol. He did so, the cold weight of the transfer hanging like implication in my hand, and then his hand fell away, the pistol was in mine, I took it out of the window, turned it upon her, and sighting the delicate wedge of neck as it glinted at me through the stones, I shot her. Blood sprang. She screamed. I shot her again. No sound, only the rush of blood now in the stillness.

The child began to cry.

Sex and death, ladies and gentlemen, death and sex, that most ancient and useful of all the equations. Dry sense of righteousness, a feeling of completion and the aridity filled with blood, I engorged hugely again, had a spontaneous orgasm, which compared to the other one was like a decapitation as against a headache, a gigantic sneeze of the genitals which toppled me and brought me to ground, and all the time I was laughing, laughing, Lawson's cries, too, like bird shrieks behind me. The laughter joined, ribboned and flowed together, and then I realized that the child was an irritant upon my consciousness; here I was, just on the afterslide of having completed a massive and significant act, and the damned child, the damned child was crying and the irritant grew, a coldness growing in the groin where warmth and flowing had been, and I felt my body assemble itself again. The pistol was still in my hand. (Stupidly in laughter I had fallen upon it; I might have discharged it, I might have killed myself, this is some measure of the ultimate ineptness of what I had done and I hope that this brief will be held for me in the times to come.) I turned it upon that little sobbing form in the darkness and discharged it once more.

And again.

The thing babbled like a bird and was still, one feeble thrash and it was gone. I went toward it to see the thing that I had killed, ancient pride and lust mingling just as the Institute had always predicted would be the case when we got into the enforcement procedures, and turned it over then with a toe, looked at the blank little face, the stricken little eyes, flush of cheek, hover of lip; the thing could not have been more than three years old. In another five it would have been ready for the bands itself, if it had not been carved up and eaten for fodder. Either way, I had done a service. I had certainly done a service. I turned the form over again, replacing it in the mire, and walked back to the car.

Lawson awaited me and there I would like to say that we committed yet one more act, one that would finalize and quantify all that had preceded, but we did not, it would be fiction, not fact, saying that this was undergone, because the truth was that I was absolutely fucked out and there was nothing to do but slump behind the wheel, pistol and prick dangling for a while, while slowly the great wheel of my senses reordered itself against the night and the engine chugged slowly, slowly back to life, and the car rolled on, on, on.

x

In Death and Disorder One-Oh-Four I remember being told in an early lecture that the first kill, when we assumed our positions and went into the Network to enforce, might well change our lives. "You will not be the same again," the lecturer had warned us through the application of old tapes which had, as I recall, a rather Mediterranean accent, "no matter how bloodlessly you seek to perform your duties, no matter how aseptic the job of the Enforcer, you will find that the first kill, and it will surely come, is difficult for obvious reasons. You will have to deal with the understandable feelings of guilt and rage which are provoked by this. You will have to grapple with your natural misapprehension that those in the Network are human and the kill is a murder. You must be made aware of these factors now; there is nothing shameful or inexact about these reactions, but by knowing you will be able to deal with the problem—shortly you will find the kills quite bearable, even enjoyable.

"But the first kill is a blooding. You are merely the latest in the succession of a very long and honorable profession, that of the mercenary who defends the borders of his land, saves the citizens from peril, sacrifices his life for the safety of those citizens—and through every era, through all the generations of man, the mercenary has been misunderstood, maligned, suffered humiliation; it is true that at various historical periods the momentary abolition of the mercenary class in various societies was accomplished by those against them achieving brief power.

But every time, every time that this happened—that the mercenaries were removed from their noble and ancient posts—the crumbling of the society came soon thereafter. *Without Enforcers to maintain order there is no order.* The megalopolis of the nineteen-eighties nearly perished for precisely this reason; this technocracy came at the conclusion of almost a century without a defined class of mercenaries . . . and only the social awareness, belated but real, of this problem, the reconstitution of the mercenary class, saved our world.

"So that first kill, that first ancient joining of the blood, joins you to an even older, a far more honorable history than you may ever know. Your first kill will be the end of your apprenticeship, your fullest initiation into the honorable and timeless role of the mercenary . . . and you should look upon the kill in that way."

Well, I did. I certainly had nothing against the idea of killing from the start; what would be the point of an Enforcer, after all, if there were no killing to be done? But Lawson has not reacted in this way; some faint weakness, a fault vein, has been magnified within him and it is now obvious that he cannot deal with the implications of what we have done.

Fuck him.

It is not necessary for him to deal. His role from here onward is that of passive speculator in chances. If there are challenges to be met then I will meet them, for I have become an Enforcer. Clearly the kill has changed my personality for the better; note the dramatic acceptance of my responsibilities.

Huge chunks of expository material swarm before me as I drive the Cadillac over the shores of west New York, looking at the dim, blasted memory of New Jersey across the shore, still unrestored from the great sweeps of the nineties. Foreground: This cinema, my life, is foreground, but there is a history to this world, this mess, this Institute, the Network.

Network.

What is the origin of Network?

"Network," the lecturer says, rolling himself on his little plastic wheels across the stage, "Network as a distinct way of life, as a category, is almost a century and a half old, make that two centuries at the present time, but it became fit material for the Enforcers of the Institute only in the nineteen-nineties, the seeds of this possibility having been sown in the sixties. Life accelerates, one hundred and fifty years of urbanization and technology to uncover the disaster, twenty more years sharp ride down, now every year counts and the mighty Institute, its great armaments, control all of the landscape." The lecturer jiggles and bobbles, assumes a curiously lifelike posture underneath the strobe, looking almost as if it were reaching for a cigarette. "It certainly was tough in the cities in those years," he confides, "consider, consider."

Consider indeed: Now the Network is closed to all but highly approved Institute personnel and those officials of the government who on occasions they will escort. Network is the terrain of the Institute; it is possible for the ground to be swept clean in a wide area before the visit of any state official, but these visits are often at the level of surprise inspections, making Institute personnel scurry, you can be sure. Would the list of approved visitors to the Network include Lawson and myself? It is a dark question and one that I cannot easily explore; I must lift it tenderly at the edges like a piece of undone meat to spot the dark patches of completion below.

"Institute personnel control the Network," the lecturer points out helpfully. "Students of the Institute are not permitted beyond the barriers except in great times of revolution or tumult when they may be conscripted as emergency forces. The reasons for this are several: to protect the integrity of the Network, to protect the integrity of the Institute, and to protect the inhabitants of Network themselves, subscribers no less than the mercenaries themselves to that ancient and honorable tradition which holds that various ways of life must be sealed off from one another; a celebration of pluralism, the protection of opposites . . . and the tenants of the Network are entitled to their territory. It is the sole assignment of Institute personnel to maintain the barriers and to maintain order in the Network . . . but the tenants are entitled to the integrity of their own lives."

Entitled to the integrity of their own lives: It is an exciting thought, a new realization; suddenly the ancient rules and creeds of the Institute flame within me and I understand exactly what the lecturers have been talking about.

We are not enforcing a way of life; we are simply maintaining a separation.

The insight is amazing; I groan, I gasp, I lose control over the wheel, the car sways, it moves from one side of the road to the other side, suspension crackles . . . and Lawson is gibbering, motioning frantically at the windshield of the car.

He is trying to tell me something, I turn toward him then, literally desperate to understand what he is saying. His forehead bulges as if with information to be imparted . . . and then the road falls away from us with the grace of discarded clothing. It falls away and we skitter, *wham, rumpty bump!* down a hundred feet of stone to dead, leveled land, the Cadillac absolutely out of control, Lawson, uppers or not, screaming, and I return to the wheel, shaking and twisting it as a floundering man might struggle with a shark; I spin the wheel, grind the clutch, pump the brakes, all of the gestures quite helpless. And we are still rolling, jogging on the earth at thirty miles an hour, the power brakes squeezing, squeezing through their vacuum reservoirs, and finally we plunge upon an abutment with a crash which sends me into the dashboard and back again, into it and back again, bouncing between dash and seat like a squash ball run amuck, until finally the heaving of that great vomiting animal, the car, comes to a pause.

We come to rest. The windshield bears a long crack now which filters into little tubers throughout its full length, those tubers each carrying their bright message of blood. I put hand to forehead, feel the small cut, press back against it. My head surges with pain, the senses reel and reorder themselves. I make gagging sounds. Little scrambling noises come from underneath the hood as if a horde of insects there had been unleashed by the collision.

Lawson moves over, galvanized into action, his face streaked by moisture but otherwise unmarked. He reaches over and tries to start the car, wheeling the key in the ignition, cursing as the mechanism fails to respond. Our disaster seems to have revivified him, as though he had found the proper confirmation that we have been destroyed. His eyes look clearer than they have for a long time; panic no longer leaps and perks at the folds of his skin like a school of trapped fish.

"Finished," he says quietly enough. "Now we're finished. I could have told you that. I always knew that it would work out this way."

"Don't panic," I say.

I move my hand off the forehead again, uncover another smear of blood upon the hand, but the imprint is not as deep nor the blood so luxuriously colored. I will myself toward control, test various surfaces of the familiar, almost-as-good-as-new body, finding that other than the cut on the forehead I appear to be uninjured. Limbs flex, blood runs, the mind begins to move once again. I jam a hip into him, sprawl him away.

"Now just stay calm," I say. "We're not in any serious trouble at all."

"That's for you to say. That's for you to say." He stretches on the seat almost luxuriously, clasping his hands, leaning all the way back. "As far as I'm concerned we're finished now." The discovery does not seem to cause him undue concern. "This was crazy," he says. "It was crazy from the beginning."

"We're in control of this as long as we stay in control, just remember that. We've got the guns and we know our way."

"How are we going to get out of here now?" He does not sound concerned about this; it is more of a detached inquiry about another person, some member of the Institute who long ago overreached himself and found difficulty. "What have you done to us?" he says.

"Don't turn it on me. It was a shared idea. We worked on this together."

"You. All the time you. I hate you," Lawson says flatly. "I really do."

"That's hardly constructive," I say, "and besides, I'm sure that we'll find a way." Otherwise I ignore the accusation. It is a matter of indifference to me how Lawson feels; my own emotions are not affectionate. It is true that he is indeed the younger of us, the difference is only a couple of months, to be sure, but still significant until one has at least lurched past the age of twenty-five. He, then, is a child, despite all of his seeming attitudes, and probably destroyed by the kill while I have been ennobled. I am aware that I must function not only for myself but for him. If I am the stronger, then the mission depends upon me.

I turn, dabbing at my wound once again, feeling the dry threads of scab already beginning to pry at my fingers. So rapid a healing; the body has its own design. "All we have to do is to get to a checkpoint," I say. "We have our credentials. Once we make a checkpoint we'll be shielded by barrier personnel until we're picked up and taken back to the Institute."

"They'll kill us," Lawson says.

"Where?"

"At the Institute. We're out without leave. They'll throw us out."

"No they won't," I say, although this is a new thought, something to be considered. "We can't possibly be such an unusual case. Many have done it. They'll understand; we'll just be confined to the end of the year."

"No, we won't," Lawson says, "no, no, we won't; they're going to ruin us. We can't go to a barrier. Somehow we've got to get back there without being discovered."

"Run the checkpoint?" I say. Cautiously I open a door; insects jab at me in the darkness. It gulps at me. "I don't think we can run a checkpoint."

"What's our choice?" Lawson says. "What's our position? To sit in the barrier and wait for them to haul us in?" He opens his own door; there is a similar attack of insects from his side but he does not retreat. Instead, he works his way out, holds onto the roof for balance, turns to face me, both hands flat on the roof. "I don't care what you do," he says, "I don't give a fuck what you do, but I can tell you about me. I'm going to try to strike my way. I'm going to get back there."

"We're twenty miles down."

"Have to do it," Lawson says. The man is crazed. Obviously conditions have completely toppled his intelligence and now he is barely able to function. "And you know what?" he says, lowering himself to speak into the car. "I'll tell them that it was all your fault. I'll tell them that it was your idea, that you were behind the whole thing. You know what? I'm going to turn you in, now how do you like that? I'll tell them that it was your fault."

He turns, he staggers once again, then, in an erratic, weaving gait, he begins to pick his way from the car and into the darkness. I hear noises slamming somewhere between us and quickly the sound overtakes his footsteps.

Mad, obviously mad, but here is a new madness. Here is a new insanity to compound our already difficult trip. I sit in the car and look out in his direction for only an instant, and then slowly I heave myself from position, out into the blasted night to pursue him, knowing that the primary danger Lawson presents is to himself and that any action is better than no action.

xi

It is as if Abraham Zapruder—the sainted and vital photographer-teacher-historian himself—is snapping off in sequence a series of snapshots of my life.

Zapruder One: I emerge into the cooperative howling, a healthy, bouncing child indistinguishable from the thousands of others born on that day, except for a slight oxygen deficiency, blueness almost instantly rectified by dedicated staff.

Zapruder Three Thousand and Fifteen: I am informed on my sixteenth birthday that testing is negative and that no clear definition of specialty has been accomplished, no simple aptitude has been devised; it is possible that I will be forced at the age of eighteen to leave the cooperative to take my chances upon winning my way back from the Network.

Zapruder Three Thousand and Fifteen, et seq: Various desperate efforts of the indigent but deeply affecting youth to discover a specialty, some apitude, are rebuffed, end in failure; gloom, sweats, chills, and self-revulsion set in.

Zapruder Four Thousand Five Hundred: A sudden vacancy appears at the last moment in the Institute; almost too late for enrollment, news of that vacancy is sped to me; I hasten to enlist, I submit myself to questioning, I submit myself to tests, my finely quivering, palpitating face showing both sensitivity and fright as I await the verdict.

Zapruder Four Thousand Seven Hundred and Two: I am informed of eligibility for the Institute; I am invited to enroll in the Institute; I immediately embark upon my career in the Institute, pausing only to seize certain vital but secret materials from the cooperative.

Zapruder Five Thousand and Seven: I team up with Lawson; we become a team, a little band, as it were, assembled to spend our years together.

Zapruder Five Thousand and Twelve, et. seq: Various pornographic scenes too dull and repetitive to mention, having to do with intertwined limbs, much huffing and puffing.

Zapruder Six Thousand and Four, et. seq: The training goes well, the auspicious youth is grounded in the lore and traditions of the Institute; he grows and matures under its vigorous programs, he dedicates himself to the life of the mercenary soldier.

Zapruder Six Thousand and One: I make my decision to attempt the illicit journey into Network; Zapruder crouches, he is running out of film, yet nevertheless he desperately applies himself.

Zapruder Six Thousand and Seven: The tormented but always sympathetic protagonist engages in an act of sexual intercourse with a female denizen of the Network; spitework perhaps, later he feels guilty.

Zapruder Six Thousand and Fourteen: Zapruder is now out of film, he is no longer able to record the images, nevertheless, linked to the camera, his only tenuous hold upon reality, he keeps on flicking and snapping away, putting blankness into the empty chambers; he is unable to straighten, he is periscoped into attention, he cannot, no matter how he tries, manage to inscribe the events, yet he cannot stop either . . .

"Screw this," Zapruder says, finally coming to his senses after a long time, flinging away the camera and walking almost gaily onto the grassy knoll. "It's not my affair, it's not my responsibility, I don't have to sit still for this crap anymore."

xii

Pausing in my flight after Lawson, I turn, go back slowly to the car, stand by the hood. It is quite impossible to track him in this darkness, and furthermore I am overtaken by a sudden and total disinterest. What does it matter? What is the difference, anyway? He could not possibly get back to the Institute, and even if he did he would not be in a position to call down retribution upon me.

No, I must find my own course.

Little ropes of steam are coming from their places of concealment under the hood, flickers of pain in my legs and belly. Still, it cannot be said that I feel seriously at bay. Truly I do not. The situation has now reached the point so rapidly where the outward disaster has long since confirmed all premonitions; now there is nothing to do but to give up and go with it. Our folly is so catastrophic as to be exhilarating. Things could be worse, I think, we could both be dead, or at least *I* could be dead; it would not matter so much what happened to Lawson, although his dying would be a mild convenience.

As if in confirmation of this, or maybe I am thinking of denial, Lawson emerges from the darkness walking straight toward me, still in that stumbling gait, an abashed expression on those portions of his face that I can see, his pistol in his hand held straight down, pointed toward the ground. He is shaking his head.

"No use," he says, "there's no use. It's straight mud all the way up, do you know that? It's impassable. The only way to get through is the road."

"Of course," I say, "that was the way it was planned."

"All right," Lawson says. He seems to have cultivated,

or is trying to cultivate, a desperate reasonableness. "I'm sorry I said I would turn you in. I'd never turn you in; how could I do that? The point is how are we going to get out of here? How will we save ourselves?" He puts his pistol inside of his pants, shrugs, looks down again in that abashed way. "You realize I didn't mean a word of any of this," he says. "I was just trying to shock you."

Of course. I examine the terrain keenly. There is little to see, but what I have learned of the Network through institutional perceptions adds as it were a whole range of color and perception, and it is as if I see not only these shores but all of the difficult history, the animals beneath the surface. Dead forms bulking in the water, shapes that might be human corpses bulging on the waterline. They do not bury their dead but simply dispose of them. Around the pillar are larger shapes which might be rotting automobiles, all edges and ruined glass; I would not go there to investigate. At one time automobile use in the Network had not been restricted and it was a prevalent means of transportation. The sweep took care of that, of course. The sweep took care of almost everything. Artifacts, artifacts, all of them frozen in time as if they had existed for centuries and the damned world so quiet. We might be artifacts ourselves frozen into the gelatinous pit of this place. A no-man's-land, a dead area, too far north apparently for a glimpse of those rioters who had so excited the young guard but too far west to be part of Westerly. What could it be? "They must have sabotaged the highway," I say, quite judiciously and calmly under the circumstances. "Sooner or later that was bound to happen. They're quite clever. We'll have to report it when we get back; this area is going to have to be sealed off."

"Wrecked the highway?" Lawson says.

He is eager to please once again, but with this benign attitude the fear has returned. I do not know which I prefer—a cooperative Lawson afraid of his life and on the verge of dissolution, or an angry, self-preserving

Lawson who would as soon destroy me as well. I do not think that this constitutes much of a choice.

"What do you mean, they wrecked the highway?" he repeats.

"Trapped it out," I say. "Put pilings on it, or maybe just cut it away. They must have more advanced technology than we calculated," I say musingly. "They must have torches of some sort."

"That was their plan from the beginning, then," Lawson says, his eyes bulging savagely. "They knew all along that we were going to come here; they screwed up the highway so that we would fall into their hands."

"Shut up."

"They're watching us. They're watching us right now. I feel their eyes on us."

"I said shut up." His nervousness and fear are actively repellent. I can smell him. "Go on, strike your way back to the Institute. Report me, just get out of here."

"I'm not going into that," Lawson says. "There's no way that I'm going to get into that. I tell you, I feel them! They're probably in the water right now, just bobbing around. Laughing!"

Once more he reaches for the gun, although the tremor of his hands is such that now he can barely hold it. He lifts it above his waist with difficulty. "I'll take some of them with me anyway!" he screams. "I'm not afraid. I'm not afraid of the scum down here. Do you hear that, scum? I'm not afraid of any of you!"

I seize his arm. "Now stop it!" I say, "just stop it!"

But his eyes, those damned eyes, are rolling and quivering, almost squeezing out of his head, his body seemingly a trembling appendage attached to those eyes. . . . And then he makes a half lunge toward me, raising the pistol as he does so. His plans seem to have something to do with shooting me in the neck, although one could not say that there is within him an excess of determination. He sighs, he groans, his body comes against mine, almost swaddling it as he begins to work on the pistol.

Enough. Really, I am quite out of patience with him; these violent swings of mood are not doing us any good and it is impossible to deal with our perilous circumstance reasonably if I must, all the time, be concerned with whether Lawson is dependent or aggressive. The very threads of his personality, assuredly, have begun to snap under the pressure and the heavy pieces of that personality, beginning to break away, float like jetsam in his psyche, but this is not my concern. Hit him in the shoulder, looking for a pressure point; find it with a thumb, dig the thumb in and get in there deeply enough to temporarily paralyze. He begins to whimper as I screw my thumb around in the well of his body; I wait until that whimpering assumes what I take to be the proper note and only then do I withdraw. He flails, he moans, standing in this way before me.

"I can hurt you," I say, finding strange pride in this assertion. "I can hurt you very badly. I read manuals. I know all the sensitive areas of the human body. If you don't leave me alone I can paralyze you for life."

He rubs the shoulder, looks at me uncomprehendingly. "Help me," he says. "You've got to get me out of here now." He rubs his shoulder, revolves the joint in the socket, crying from the pain. "I can't deal with this," he says, "I just can't cope. It isn't right for you to make me deal with it. Get me out of here."

"I'll help," I say, "I'll help you. You can trust me and I'll get us through; stop whimpering, stop squealing around," although my impulse, lamentable as it might be, is to abandon him right where we stand, on the lip of Southway. Let him deal for himself. Not only has the kill made me a mercenary in truth, it has almost mystically changed the chemical composition of my blood and his. We are not the people that we were. Something between us is now finished. That impulse to leave him is easily understood in light of this . . . but it would be regrettable soon enough. I would not appreciate this. His lone, staggering form would soon bring the bands upon him and then me, and for the bands we would be an easy pair of kills. I do not think that they would spare us, nor do I think myself capable of dealing with a pack of forty or fifty inhabitants. My exhilaration is profound but at the core of it is a cool dispassion. I do not overestimate my new gifts nor do I misjudge situations. The kill has lent me discipline, a controlled view of the world. Network is dangerous. It is very dangerous. I am now aware of the parameters.

So I say, "Come on, then. Stay with me. We're going to stick to the waterline and move fast. It leads straight up to Northing, twenty miles or so; if we move along and don't have any trouble we might see it by daybreak. Four hours, five hours, if you can move."

"My shoulder hurts. I can't move fast because of the pain."

"You'll move fast," I say. I extend a hand, touch him in the afflicted part, and he whimpers again. "You'll move fast or I'll hurt you again."

I release the grip, turn from him. Momentarily ignoring him I strike a firm and determined pace away. The ground is rutted but reasonably steady, small objects are deeply embedded within that terrain, but surprisingly it responds better to a fast pace than to a slow one, it being possible to literally skim over the little obstructions. I hear him wheeze and pant behind me. I hear him gather speed as he, too, learns the lessons of the terrain. Slices of light, penetrating from the pitched camps on the Jersey shore (another locale, another Institute, a part of life which is to me utterly foreign), knife across and I am able to see, in that brief flash, straight up the river toward the ruined bridge, and beyond it Northing. In that glimpse all things seem possible, dreams, flight, history intermingling, and I know that we will reach the bridge and we will be safe. We will be at the barriers well before dawn.

The odors come up stronger in a harsh burst of wind.

Corpses, animals, the smells of the river itself mingle in my nostrils, giving a sudden lurch of poignancy; it is terrible what has been done to this terrain. It is really too bad that Network has become Network; it must have been quite a remarkable place several hundred years ago, must have offered a most gentle and bucolic existence.

We pick our way, Lawson and me, along the waterfront plankings some twenty miles, as far as we can judge it, to the north. A foolish journey, a doomed journey. How do we presume to make twenty miles through this dread and hostile terrain when we cannot move even a few feet without slipping and sliding to the ooze? But I have managed to persuade Lawson of the sanity of this course, so he will not protest. Who would he be to protest at this point? Protestations would have been for a while ago.

Suddenly, there are forms before us.

All of this happens so quickly that it is impossible to spot a point of transition, to make of all this a hereness separated from the time when there was no one standing before us and we were moving undeterred. Like brushes in the landscape itself, darting across the seat of consciousness, the forms appear: five of them, six of them, coming out against the land, lift their arms, bring us to a halt. They are carrying, we can clearly see, weapons in those hands.

Bands. The bands of Westerly.

We stand there. The pistols are in our hands, or at least inside clothing, but that would be pointless; it would be as foolish to take up arms against these bodies in front of us as to start lighting small fires in the ooze. The fires would blaze and bank out against the pilings just as we would be broken against the bands. So we only stay there, we only stand there in solemn frieze, jammed up now against a wall which had tracked to our right and Lawson is saying over and over again: "Oh my God, now we're really finished. We're really finished now. Look what they've done to us. Look what has happened to us. Oh, we'll never get out of this now."

Oh yes, yes, this is what I admire most about Lawson. His calm under pressure. The failure of his personality to splinter under stress. The way in which, time and again, he will yield to even the most inglorious of predicaments that special and calm overlay, that slender, cold pipe of truth through which all calm and recovery may pass.

xiii

It has occurred to me, on at least one occasion anyway, that all of this which I have constructed may be a dream and that the extrinsic reality may be something far more grim and deadly. Who is not to say, I thought once, looking up at the smooth, clear dome of the Institute, that grey, sweeping, inverted concourse that hung over us, protecting us from all outside pressures and influences, that everything that they have told us is a series of lies or, better yet, a dream; that there is no Network outside, that there is nothing to the south of us whatsoever but merely a bland assemblage of machinery, programmed a long, long time ago to tell us such lies in accordance with the instructions of long-deceased programmers? This thought occurred to me, the unreality of the Institute; that is to say, the fact that so much of our apprehension of the Network was constructed upon hearsay, but I discarded it. I put it aside. What good would it do, after all, to speculate upon the possible unreality of our situation, to open up the doors of a trap, a long, spiraling excursion into some tunnel of mystery at the end of which . . . well, at the end of which would probably still exist the Network itself.

Why not? Whether the Network is a state of being or a state of mind, the central truth of that construction will always hold. Why not face up to it? The Network is what we have created; it is the necessary waste of the technologized society; it can be explained as machine loss, the difference that is between energy input and output as disguised in the appearance of useless materials. There was always a Network in our future, this is what the Institute has made clear to us; at the end of post-industrialization were these wasted spaces, and whether we found them in reality or dreams, whether the world ended or merely crested to a state of abeyance while underneath Network tugged and tugged away . . . what be the difference?

So what I am saying is this: That all that I have related to have occurred may not have; that the expedition to Network may be a construct; that Lawson himself may be some figment of my highly disordered imagination, just as the lecturers in the great Institute itself, the crevices and materials of the Institute, may yet be imaginary. . . . But what is there to say? Is the pain any more reduced? Is the situation any less ominous or terrible simply because it may not exist and the world itself may have ended in the year two thousand fifty-three, years ago, exactly as was predicted by so many of the prophets of the post technological era? Real or unreal pain still hurts, blood still runs, corruption and darkness still rise to overtake all of us, and upon that simple assumption are these painful memoirs themselves based. No matter what the other consequences, in short, life, even if it is only known as death, must go on and on that pretext must one continue. It is possible that I have lied about Lawson. It is possible that I may have lied about my relationship to Lawson. It is highly possible that buggery and blood, the intertwined mysteries of the flesh as I have recounted them, may never have happened but that all the time, all of it, it had been me alone and Lawson merely the projection of my disordered but still lively consciousness.

But what difference? What difference all of it? The winds still rise, the mud oozes, the dark shape of New Jersey probes its way through the vapors to reveal and disreveal itself in the fog, and all of it must continue to the preordained end; unless, of course, it does not continue, which would render matters an entirely different case but one which I would not care to discuss at the present time. Later, the situation may change, of course.

It always, always does.

xiv

So, backed against the fences lining the river now, pressing our little joints into those damp and welcoming slats, Lawson and I are being closed off by by a band from Westerly. I know that they are Westerly for they wear the insignia of the area: The legions of the *W*. (All of the bands have the separate markings of their sections; haven't I said that before? Of course I have said that before, or at least I should have pointed it out, that Southways are marked with an *S*, Northings with an *N*, Eastos with the big *E*, and so on and so forth, this giving them a feeling of identity, the psychology of the pack. So we were told anyway in the Institute, so at least it was stated to us, that the bands wore their identification at all times because it gave them a feeling of bonding. I am hardly going to quibble with the teachings of the Institute and besides, big as life, big as death, I see upon them the insignia stating *W* and have nothing more to say about the issue. Do not test my credibility upon such frail grounds as this.)

Backing against the fence, my little buttocks trembling with rage and apprehension (I do not look at Lawson at this time; I have my own problems), it comes back to me that the teachings state the Westerly bands are the most dangerous of all. Their terrain makes it necessary, we have been told, for them to learn water navigation as well as how to scurry on land, and this water-knowledge, this piscine facility, as I would put it, enables them to voyage from their limited territory into the range of the other bands even as the very dangerous and virulent gangs of Northing cannot. The Westerlys can strike at Northing, hit Southway and its *S*'s a devastating blow, still circling come in on Easto . . . oh, it can be terrible. Indubitably, they are the most dangerous because the most mobile of all the various bands of Network.

They are not, looking at these faces I can see this, ageless like the older tenants of Northing; they have none of the aspect of the man and woman with whom we have dealt earlier this event-packed evening, but instead fit quite neatly into an age level which, not without some irony, seems to be quite close to our own. In fact they might even be a little younger.

"Ho there!" one says somewhat floridly and then breaks into a series of uneven giggles, "stop right there, gentlemen!" He must be the leader, at least he is the one in front of them in that pack and point information which they have adopted (it is always surprising to see something come out exactly as teachings have promised) into which they naturally fall. "Ho there!" he says again, apparently pleased with the floridity of his expression. He gestures, his limbs falling smoothly, evenly against one another; certainly far more graceful than we might have suspected. "We want to talk to you."

"God," Lawson says. "God, God," he says again and reaches within his belt, obviously looking for the gun, but he does the reaching with the shoulder that I have injured. Remembering this he groans, gasps, stops the motion stupidly as if trying to relocate the parameters of his body. I wonder how I could have ever found him attractive. "Oh my God, this isn't right, this can't be—"

"Stop it, you fool," I say. The leader closing in on us smiles, enjoying the disagreement. "We emptied the guns into the ground, remember?"

"Oh no, we—"

"Don't take out the gun!" I shout. I am no longer concerned whether or not the pack hears this; it is my own preservation in which I am interested. "Don't show them; they'll kill us for it on the spot."

"Sensible," the leader says, "that's all very sensible thinking."

"Just try to remember," I say more quietly, "that we are not offering you any harm. We are merely trying to find our way to the checkpoint."

This seems to strike the leader as humorous, or at least he responds to this with a quizzical upturn of the eyebrows, quite a subtle gesture indeed, considering his otherwise rather menacing posture and the difficult situation in which we find ourselves, but before he has an opportunity to make his position known on the situation, Lawson is babbling again. Really, the man is quite out of control.

"We were going to refill the guns," he is saying, "oh my God, God" (again he seems to be invoking a plethora of deities), "we were going to *refill,* we meant to do that, didn't we, it was such a simple thing; I can't stand this any more! I'm so afraid," he mumbles, clutching me with his uninjured arm, "so terribly afraid. Run, please, we have got to run out of here, oh please, we must—"

Repellent. At best the situation is now intolerable; I cannot judge how many there are in this band, ten, twelve, perhaps, all clustered unspeaking behind the leader, but certainly sufficient here to outwit and overpower. But at least I am entitled to the dignity of confrontation, the small chance that I might be able to deal with these people, manipulate them into some understanding of my superiority and the heinous revenge which the Institute itself will wreak against any group that would injure their personnel . . . but with Lawson mumbling and babbling away it is quite impossible, quite impossible to do anything. Really, he is barely a parody of himself, leaning against me, gelatinous in his ruined clothing, croaking his little sobs and pleas, and I remember once again the litany of the Institute: Some will grow from the kill, others will shrink from it, the terms of the mercenary are terrible and eternal but the imprint will remain forever. Ritual comes back easily in times of stress; this is precisely its purpose. One would think.

"Shut up," I say to him, "shut up now." I hit him in the mouth.

The abused mouth, the tormented shoulder must mesh; he screams. How could I have ever felt desire for this individual? I cannot even bear to look at him. He puts his little strands of appendages on me, mouth wide open, and says, "You shouldn't, you shouldn't—" and I cut him off with another clout to the cheek. Finally, finally, he falls away from me. He penetrates the mud, lies there flopping.

Headlights are suddenly perceived in the darkness. They flick in the distance, insects swarming in their center. "We found their car," a voice says and then the lights go off. The leader turns, looks, then inverts back to me. "So that's how you came," he said. He puts a hand on chin, stares at me meditatively. In this posture he looks vaguely like Lawson, as do all the shapes behind him, shapes on the shores of Westerly; is all my life then to be composed of the one form endlessly repeated? Surely there must be more variation to life than that. He is laughing, the leader, the laughter crawling out of him in little ropes of sound. Then he reaches into his pocket and when his hand withdraws he, too, is holding a gun."

"That's quite enough," he says. He talks a perfect, flat, unaccented tongue, the sound of the Network. "Quite enough," he says, looking down at Lawson in the ooze. "You sons of bitches are going to face judgement now." Truly, the threat seems as mechanical and reproduced as his accent itself, but on the other hand Lawson shakes on the ground, lending it a credibility which I must share. "Just rest in place," he says, "rest in place," breaking on on the *place,* his voice suddenly youthful, and it occurs to me that the leader of this attacking band is probably no older than Lawson or myself, which is probable since the lifespan of the bands in the Network cannot be very high, even for the leaders. Mostly for the leaders. They are, after all, fully grown at twelve, the Network forcing maturity upon them so that by their midteens they have achieved full virulence and physical maturity . . . and then they die at twenty-five or so, usually by violence.

"Just rest in place," the leader says again. He seems to be pleased by the phrase, it gives him some obscure comfort. "After all," he says, "after all, you must understand that you can't get away with this, and besides that, you know we're going to kill you." He adds this offhandedly, virtually in an apologetic tone of voice. It is not that killing is necessary, his tone seems to indicate, so much as it is an unhappy action to which he will be reluctantly forced. It is the voice of one of the advisors in the Institue. I don't want to kill you, I expect to hear him add, but then again you wouldn't be happy unless we did; after all, that's the promise of interception. He does not add this, however, he does not add anything at all, and I understand that much of this I have constructed, after a fashion, in my head and there is not much to be expected of the objective reality of the situation. It is very difficult to make demands upon objective reality; it has all that it can do to sustain itself at the miserable level at which it has been inaugurated.

It cannot be happening, I think. This cannot possibly be happening. Lawson lies on the ground curled in upon himself, as sodden and invisible as a piece of vegetation. Little purrs and sniffles come from his open mouth, otherwise he is out of the situation. The breath, that ancient burden, must continue up to the point of impact. It cannot be happening. I put my hands at sides, palms exposed, risk a glance at the river. Cannot, cannot, cannot be going on and yet I know better, dreams do not have the veracity which this possesses.

(I cannot through all of this escape the belief in some pocket of the consciousness that the Institute has kept a benign watch upon us from the very beginning. That they have tracked our path from barrier to checkpoint to Northing to Westerly, smiling their indulgent supervisory smile, and that when we have been taught a good lesson, when in the judgement of the Institute we have rendered ourselves incapable of such further disobedience, then a full patrol in the garb of the Enforcers will spring from a clump of ooze somewhere to the background and effect a dramatic and bloodly rescue, scattering the members of the band about as they rush in to save us. This is a lamentable way of thinking—it denies, among many other things, any consequence or responsibility—but I do not think that I can be fully blamed for sustaining such dreams. The perils of a protected upbringing, the belief that at any given time one can be rescued, that one is too uniquely valuable to ever get into real trouble. Certainly, since I entered the Institute I have had a protected upbringing. The belief that we may be saved may be unreasonable, but surely, surely, I am thinking, the Institute, which has invested so much in our training, could not abandon us now. Not in terms of that cost invoked, not in terms of our unique and genuine value. The knowledge we have gained of Network in our unauthorized expedition, the knowledge we have gained of ourselves . . . well, could not this all somehow be a quest mission, part of the training itself? Surely they will rescue us. In any event, this is the quality of my speculation. This memoir is entitled to be complete. I will say everything that has to be said, even if it is to my occasional discredit. One must set down the facts truly. From this memoir will come great successes, and even if I am indeed doomed the memoir will live on. I cannot understand these excesses of self-justification but I am sure that you can, you can, and that you will be merciful. We are too precious to risk. Far too valuable for casual abandonment. I do believe this.)

Lawson is raving, shrieking, mumbling on the ground. The man, literally, will not be quiet. "Please," he is saying now, "please don't hurt me. Don't do anything to me, it was all his idea, deal with him," and a feeble claw, stained with ooze, reaches out of the ground to thrust toward me. I could have expected nothing else, I stand my ground. "He did it, all of it."

"No I didn't," I say, applying an essential corrective

before the lie can increase, "it was both of our ideas, and anyway, all of the time I was caught by his influence. On my own I wouldn't have done any of it."

"He took us in here," Lawson says, not cognizant of my wise and irrefutable statement of the facts, "he took us in here, not me, he made us do the deeds, do you know what he did? He killed a child, he raped a woman, he killed a man. He is a beast. I wouldn't let him get away with any of this, if you want to protect the Network you can't let people like this go around, can you? Can you?" He flops around the barren ground, considers it would seem, rising to his feet, then gives up on that difficult idea and remains on his belly, presenting a low target. "Everything was his decision," he says, "he did it all from the start, I was merely along. He forced me. He forced me at gunpoint, do you hear?"

Ah, well. It is necessary for me to strike him again merely to bring this to an end, and so I kick him hard in the face, using the toe of my highly polished Institute standard-issue boot, hearing the crack of cheekbone, feeling the spatter of blood in the hidden spaces below, and invert him that way into the mud. Still, even as he reacts, turns from the blow, he is babbling, whispering dreadful little confidences of betrayal. I think of stepping on his head but decide not to do it; this, after all, would fall within the authority sector of the leader of the band and I would not like to take away from his range and control. Of course if I killed Lawson their attention would also focus fully upon me, this is something which must definitely be considered.

At last and finally he keeps quiet, the blood drifting into the various cavities of the body shutting him off from the powers of locution. He keeps on breathing, his body stirs, but he says nothing whatsoever. The breath, that betrayer, that sneeze and twitch of the corpus against all odds, will always continue.

The leader looks at me, the remainder of the band drawing off. In this close focus there is a tunnel of concentration that moves from him to me, a black tube of connection in which only the two of us exist. Once again there is no background, only foreground. His eyes have a message and that message involves his understanding that I am the stronger of the two of us. No longer the receptacle but the conveyor. Slowly, dreadfully, he winks.

"What do you want?" he says quietly.

"I want nothing. I want to get back to the checkpoint." I exclude Lawson from this response. Truly, I am now negotiating only for myself.

"Why did you come here, then? Why have you come into our territory?"

The bands are extremely protective of their terrain, feeling it is theirs, and truly I cannot argue with them on this point. If a social group is alienated from the main benefits and flow of society, given the remains, then it is inevitable they they will assume the same attitude about that which they have been left as they assume is felt by the excluding majority. "Sociology and Sociopathology of The Network Eighty-Three," of course. Still, the precepts hold.

"We didn't mean to be here at all," I say, "we were looking for the Westerly checkpoint."

I hear the engine of the Cadillac, huddled at some point of invisibility, mumble. One of them is playing with the machinery which I have so painfully reconstituted. It is a violation, as explicit a violation of my possessions as if it were my bed with which they were playing, but there is nothing that I can do. The leader closes another few steps. He seizes me by the shirt in an old, familiar, authoritative gesture. I feel myself dive within myself.

"There is no Westerly checkpoint, you fool," he says, "there hasn't been for years."

"I thought—"

"You didn't think. You didn't think anything. We blew that one out a long time ago."

"I didn't know," I say.

"Checkpoints," the leader says, "checkpoints, barriers,

control, control, don't you people understand that you don't know what's going on here anymore? This is our territory, not yours. You haven't understood anything about this for years."

"All right," I say. I am sweating in his grip, my body writhing in confusion and fear. "Please," I say, and I too have now adopted that pleading tone that I heard to the North, "we didn't mean any harm."

"Fucking sightseers," the leader says. He dismisses me as casually as if I were an insect, leaves me in place, motions for the band to gather around him. Now, as he does so, I can see these forms, the savage and terrible forms of the Network clustered behind him, their faces glinting in the light, and never have I felt so clearly in the presence of death. The lessons of the Institute have been managed too well; I believe that they will kill me. I do not want to die. My position is certainly a limited one, I do not have much to which to look forward, but I am as entitled to my life as to the leaving of it; in either of the cases the decision should fall within my hands.

"Fucking sightseers," the leader says again and the band nods, "you're just looking for a cheap charge, you bastards, but you've got more than you—"

"No," I say, "you don't understand. It isn't that, we weren't—"

"Thrill-seekers," the leader says. His voice has assumed a rather puritan lilt, he might be working out of the Institute, "come to see the Network, come to see the freaks. But you didn't bargain for this, did you? Not bloody fucking quite."

"We're not sightseers," I say but it is useless, my words have no effect, nor do Lawson's slobbers and moans from the ground. Looking at him, digging with a toe against his skull idly much as I might push away an errant blade of grass or foliage, it occurs to me that there are limits to biter-bit; Lawson certainly deserves to have been humbled from his arrogant and domineering attitude, but I did not wish matters to go quite so far. Not so far at all.

It would be better if there were at least two of us against the band; we might be able to talk some sense into them.

"See Network," the leader says, "get a jolt, have a drag, move around, enjoy the mud, just going for a little fun dancing through the freaks, but you always get just a little more than you hype for, don't you?" Archaic slang now; they talk a jumble of all tongues, I suppose. "This is our Southway, citizen, and no sightseers come in here without full permission and tribute paid, and then we, *we* assign you a special guide to take you through."

"That's a lie," I say, "there are no guides. There is no authorization. This is outlaw territory."

The leader sneers, upper lip up. Sputum flecks his mouth, cackles in his throat. "How dare you say this? Our territory is as supervised as yours. As far as we're concerned, you're the freaks."

I look down at the ground. When there is nothing to say, say nothing then. Stand mute. Muteness is all. I shake my head. I will desist. Force control.

"Where are your credentials? Where is your permit into the Southway?"

"We have no permit. We need no permit."

"I'm going to kill you," the leader says. His gun shines by the light of a sudden torch struck behind him. The group sighs as if wind was passing through them. The torch, a pseudobattery-powered, flames away.

I try once more. "You're wrong," I say, "you don't understand anything that's going on here. We came to help you. To learn about you. To learn about your Network and—"

I decide then that I can hold back nothing. I hover on the lip of my next statement for several seconds while the leader looks at me patiently. The torch, held high behind him, burns away, sending little embers of harmlessly charged material through the night. I calculate, decide that there is nothing else to do. We hold authority over them. We are certainly entitled to better than this; of that I am sure.

"We're from the Institute," I say.

"What Institute?" someone behind the leader says. He steps out, a sullen, interested little fellow, perhaps my age, perhaps not. Rubs tiny hands together. "What shit are you talking about now?"

"What Institute?" the leader says, clapping this one on the shoulder and then restoring him to ranks. They really move in a rather tight formation; for all I know the one who asked me this is the group Questioner. There is no gainsaying the customs. "What is this Institute?" The gun dances in his fingers, then comes down toward me. "Talk, scum," he says.

I start to tell him but it is not me, it is Lawson on the ground who answers. In truth I had forgotten him, was not even aware during this latest exchange that he existed, having assigned him to some far pocket of my mind in which all of the dead are placed. "I'll tell you," he says, "I'll tell you, I'll tell you—"

"No!" I shout, not seconds ago ready to divulge all but now focused by some horrid suspicion that this would have been wrong, that imparting this information can only lead to some dreadful conclusion, lunging toward him, seeing in the frieze of that moment his face bulging, mouth opening, the eyes distended ready to impart their dreadful knowledge, hurling myself on top of him to block this disclosure but something hits me on the side of the head, some small, terrible explosion moving from the cerebral area to the impoverished and damaged heart and it is the leader's gun butt. He has struck me on the head, sent me into the sinking and stinking ooze of Southway, and I lie there, listening, listening, in the situation and yet not of it, always on the margin now.

"Tell me," the leader says, "where you come from."

"We come from the Institute for Urban Control," Lawson says flatly, dully, "the Institute for Urban Control," he says, his voice taking on a little more tone and life, perhaps being energized by the dignity of this confidence, "we come from the Institute for Urban Control!" he shrieks and something happens in the leader's hand and head, a bolt of fire seeming to weld the two, and then there is an increasing circle on the dark, brown, fading spot of Lawson's head and I see that the leader has shot him. Lawson screams, he burbles, he falls into the earth and the gun goes off again, guns in the hands of the other members of the bands similarly explode, Lawson's body is knifed by ten, twenty invasions and assaults and twitching, stitching, itching in the ooze, he rolls on his belly then and expires.

I look at all of this with some quizzicality and bemusement to be sure and then the band turns upon me.

xv

Seeing Lawson die it is as if some difficult part of my life is over; it is the surest sign that our adventures in the Network have led us to a point of irreversible dislocation from the past. Numerous scatological images float through my head in the instant and aftermath of his dying, images which are best not recounted here, but his body is one which I have probed and explored many times and it is as if the consequences of these many invasions refract back, cut into me as well, so that all the parts of me which have invaded that ruined frame are themselves burst in the multifarious abcesses of the attack. Now small holes are opened up all through the length of the body, here the prick goes, there the finger, now an ear and a toe (we have engaged in many perversions) until the fire moving up and down the span of the body literally overtakes all of me, dying with him I plunge, following the vanished parts of my body into those open spaces called death where nothing exists but desire, desire and loss conjoined, that is, and falling I do not know whether I want to live or to die, the question of survival itself, of the life-wish is careful and delicate, but the deeper I go the more I realize that I resist death and the more I resist death I become aware that I want to live, no matter how mis-spent and useless my life may become, and so like a drowner deep in the sea I break the surface screaming, screaming and thrashing for my life and the leader looks at me and I look at him, and in that glance we make a sullen and final compact which I know will be the new terms of the life that has been given back to me, and yet I am willing to take it, that life is mine, on any terms life is better than death, that is to say, and so I detach myself from the corpse of Lawson and come back to the Southway and they are still standing there and everything has changed but then again everything is still the same. This is one of the paradoxes of life.

xvi

"Institute for Urban Control," the leader says, "the Institute for Urban Control; well, we'll show you a spot for the fucking, we'll show you what your Institute means." His eyes become contemplative, he might be a much gentler man in this posture. "I always wanted to have a chance to deal with one of you," he says, "I always wanted to show you what I thought of your Institute." His gun is away, he shrugs, turns away in a convulsion of disinterest.

"Save him," he says to the group who now stand attendance upon him as if he were about to deliver a lecture of some sort, a series of abstruse academic points, that is to say, which are quite out of accordance with the brutalities of their lives in Southway, but then again you never know about things of this sort; there are more implications than can easily be explained in vision. "Save him," he says, aborting his lecture (or maybe he has merely concluded it), "I want to deal with him later, I want to have a little fun with him."

"You'll have no fun with me."

"Oh yes, I will," the leader says, "yes I will, indeed. I intend to have a good deal of fun with you. You're going to be very useful."

"Fuck you," I say. I hang onto that single strand of defiance; it is that rope which will convey me to liberation. "Fuck you all."

Quite casually, someone hits me. I feel the blow, it shakes the brain once again; colors dazzle. I will not break down. I will not break down. I do not break down.

"You'll do whatever I want you to do, you crazy, stupid, son of a bitch," the leader says, "you are completely within my hands," and then he turns and strides away, leaving me surrounded by members of the band. At some strategic point he turns, gestures, raises an arm. He really must exert some strange power upon them, they look at him most attentively. I myself have never had the ability to influence great masses of people. One to one the way I controlled Lawson, that was all. "Mop up the other one," he says, "dump him, dispose of him, clean this one up and send him to me."

part two

THE LEADER OF THE BAND

i

After we shot the first Enforcer and cleaned up and reprogrammed the second, it would be easy. The whole thing would be nothing more than a routine patrol. The trouble I had, though, getting my men to clean him up and reprogram him was irritating. They get mad early in the Institute and they stay that way.

Countershocks have to be strong.

"I am quite optimistic," I said to Five the night we trapped him. "We've been looking for one of these for a long time; now with him we'll have the means and favor to get into the Institute itself and hit them a mortal blow. Don't you think so?" leaning back easily, looking at Number Five, who is of course one of my most trusted lieutenants. Five looked back at me bleakly. "Then why kill the other one?" he said.

"To totally demoralize the one we have," I said, and then I laughed, laughed at Five to show him the ease and control which I felt, trying to impart to him a confidence which I really did not feel because, and this might as well be admitted now, I was not sure that my wild and dangerous plan would work, and if it did not then our position would be even worse than before the choice was made. Nevertheless, that choice had been made and there was nothing to do but to go ahead. Such are the risks of leadership. Sometimes it can be quite demoralizing.

Being the leader of a band in Westerly is a matter of utter dispassion. I refer to the lieutenants and followers whom I have gathered around me during the three or four years of my primacy only by numbers, and those numbers assigned in the order in which they originally joined me. Thus, Five was the fifth to join us, eighteen months ago; he came from a settlement in Easto, I believe, Easto it must have been, although generally speaking I do not care to keep an account of the members of the group which I lead and try to indulge in as little of a relationship as is possible under the circumstances.

Essentially I am dedicated to my cause, which is to assemble a striking force large enough to make an attack upon the Institute and to take over its facilities. If I can take over the facilities of the Institute, its instruction programs and grounds, its armaments and mnemonic devices, I believe then I will be able from that central point to begin the liberation of the Network itself, to come over into the Landscape. This, in any event, is my direct intention. How far, precisely, I will get with all of this I do not know, but as I have advised my forces many times, in and out of this world you only get what you dedicate yourself to having through the path of much sacrifice and what I want is to liberate the Network.

It is unfair that we should have to live in this way. It is a vicious, unequal social structure that has been carried on for too many years and it is time that it be brought down.

My point of attack is through the Institute. I see the Institute as the key to the salvage of Network, the beginning of bringing to an end the unfortunate situation in which we live. Others have worked in different ways: a frontal attack, the use of incendiaries, terrorist maneuvers, guerrilla strikes, infiltration and so on. While I pay all respect to these schools of thought, each to his own after all, it is my feeling that they are erroneous. The Institute is the soft, throbbing heart of the endeavor. It is from the Institute that the Enforcers emanate; it is the Institute itself through its films, tapes, devices, and rigid procedures which has managed for a generation to not only symbolize but to center the uneven balance of forces in which we all live. If I can seize the Institute then I believe that it will be very easy to break down the entire structure. There are, after all, so few left in positions of authority. Most of the fanatics and leadership types of the Landscape have died off. It has been left to the dead machines of the Institute to turn out the continuing generations of Enforcers, and machines are far more vulnerable than men since they cannot quickly adapt to circumstances. On the other hand, the fanatics did their job well. Regretfully I admit this. The Institute is cunningly constructed and almost impermeable.

Still, I believe if one were able to get hold of a senior trainee of the Institute, one familiar with its policies and procedures and capable of leading us into the very heart of that place where the great computer tapes which activate the machines are stored, then we would be well on our way to the liberation of the Institute and the subsequent liberation of the Landscape. At least, this is my hope. When I say "liberation of the Landscape" I am talking in a very limited sense, of course. I am no overreacher; I know my place, I know the dimensions of the problem. There are throughout this nation, I gather, some two to four hundred networks, all of them as miserably gutted and abused as ours. The country has been riven into the division between Network and the Landscape, the Enforcers functioning to keep them separate. To liberate Network is not to change the face of the nation, and so forth. Nevertheless, one must begin somewhere and thus I will start here. Liberation begins at home and etc. In the long run I have meglomaniacal ambitions, as would almost anyone in my position, but I am perfectly willing to contain them and to take matters one step at a time. In this way, I believe, lies sanity.

Exposition in place, then. "It could be very dangerous," Five said. "After all, even if they are absent from the Institute without leave it stands to reason that their comings and goings were strictly monitored. They're apt to have followed them and retaliation could be very painful."

Five has this way about him—a sniffling, snaffling,

sniveling, sneezing unwillingness to seize the moment and pursue the courageous course. Most of the members of the band are similarly constructed, although Five at least will listen to reason.

"Don't worry about it," I say, "nobody's monitoring them. This is undoubtedly a rite of passage. And in any event, we'll get him unprogrammed very easily and enough information out of him to make all of this quite routine."

"Do you believe that?" Five said. "Do you really believe that?"

"I do," I said, "and I do," and with no further words I made a gesture of dismissal, sending him from that place.

We live, or I should say we have occupied a series of bunkers and cheap cabins hurled up in what used to be Battery Park, the extreme southern tip of the Network, and as the leader of the group I am the only one entitled to separate quarters. It was in those separate quarters that I sat for quite a while pondering all of the implications of the situation, to say nothing of the florid events of the day, until Seven and Ten, using chains, brought the student Enforcer before me, the Enforcer showing a most defeated and terrified expression as would have been likely under the circumstances. Seven and Ten had been given orders to intimidate him physically and to use moderate torture, although to do nothing which would in any sense inflict permanent damage. I needed him too badly to take any risks whatsoever with his life although, of course, I did not see any need to share this knowledge with him.

"Good," I said to Seven and Ten when I had examined the gross signs of the Enforcer and had found that, as per instruction, no serious violation of bodily orifices had been accomplished. "You can leave now."

"We'd like to talk about this," Ten said. He is the youngest of the group and quite the stupidest, but also very loyal when brought about to an understanding of his duties. "We feel—"

"Later," I said, "we will discuss this later," and with a motion directed Ten out of the room. Seven had already left; he is quite well-trained, although I question his courage in a physical confrontation. We will find out about this sooner or later. "Please leave," I said to Ten. Still, he hesitated at the aperture to the bunker.

"I think you should know that he has brought us information—"

"I will find it out myself," I said, "I intend to find out the information myself," and with a violent gesture of departure indicated to Ten that he was in danger if he remained with me longer; he took the signal, he wheeled and left. The Enforcer stood before me, trembling in a light sweat, his extremities moving uneasily against the burlap he had been given to wear. "Tell me everything about the Institute," I said, "immediately. Its location, its defense perimeters, the means by which they can be assaulted. Tell me quickly."

He shook his head. One could only admire the stubbornness which existed at the center; his training may have been worthless but the discipline had been inculcated.

"No," he said, "I won't betray the Institute. I will not be an informer. Go ahead and kill me but I won't talk."

"I don't want to kill you," I said, "that would really be quite foolish and stupid. I merely wish to cooperate with you. We can help one another."

"Never," he said. He looked on the verge of fainting but held his ground. "Never," he said.

"Listen," I said, striving to be gentle, feeling that the tortures had worked on the one pole and that the other one, exposed by his listing that way, would be quite vulnerable, "it's all lies. Everything that the Institute has told you. All of the teachings. We're not the enemy. The Network isn't the enemy. The Institute is the enemy."

"Go fuck yourself."

"People opposed to the dictums and commands of the State are sent into the Network," I said, "as a means of punishment and exile. It would be easier to kill them but the State is too cowardly for mass murder; it might lead to discovery and an uprising. So people are sent into the Network, any who wish to change the status quo. But beyond that the State arbitrarily sends people to the Network for no other reason than to control the rise of population. The Networks aren't violent places. They're composed of exiles, most of whom die almost immediately because of exposure, previous tortures, lack of food. But the few strong ones who are left survive by joining the known bands or creating new ones and working against the time when they can overthrow the State. It's perfectly true. I'm telling you the empirical facts of the matter. The Networks are used as casting-off places for all those who oppose the individual states. The country has broken down into hostile and suspicious separate states, each with its own Network."

"Bullshit," he said. He was really quite strong-minded; reluctantly I found myself admiring him for this. There are very few who have come in here to stand up against the torturings of Ten and Seven who show any defiance whatsoever. It was a pity that he had to be broken but with breakage comes use, or at least this is the policy I have followed for a long time. "It's all bullshit. That's exactly what they told us to be on watch for. The rationalizations of people like you."

"But it's true," I said, standing, "it's all perfectly true," and I hit him in the mouth then, just to exercise the hand, just as punctuation to the dialogue, no real malice in it. There is no malice in any of my actions; a leader must be judicious and terror is merely another one of his range of weapons. "The cities became untenable toward the end of the twentieth century and it was decided, as governments and influential sectors of the population fled to the countryside, that they might be put to some use after all as large detention camps. From one thing to the next; now they are the absolute foundation of population control. That's all there is to it."

"I'll never believe you," he said, "no matter what you say."

"If you cooperate with us it could be much to your advantage. With the knowledge you possess, your knowledge of the Institute and its devices, I mean to say, we could make a frontal attack upon them with a very good chance of success. Once we seize the Institute we're in a good position to end this rotten, divisive situation. It's really as simple as that."

"Lies. It's all lies."

"I see that we're going to have to work to persuade you of the justice of our position," I said with some reluctance. "I really hoped that it would not be necessary to come to this. Most people are sensible but the Enforcers, I admit, are quite difficult."

"You're crazy," he said. There was some animation in his eyes for the first time; the burlap moved as he gestured. "If what you're saying is true, then why didn't the Institute fall a long time ago?"

"But it did," I say. "The Institute is fully automated, you know that. You're controlled by machinery; there are only a very few human proctors to monitor all of those devices. Actually, the Landscape is crumpling because all of the people who could run it have been exiled to the Network. It manages to continue only because of the advantage you possess in natural resources and because the revolutionary forces of the Network have been too scattered and dispersed until recently. But now everything is moving ahead quite quickly. Why not join us?" I said. "Why not be reasonable about this? It's all going to fall very quickly whether we do anything or not, just collapse of its own weight and corruption, so why don't you join us and at least take some of the credit for ending this rotten system?" I gave him my most winning smile. "I'm really sorry that we had to kill your friend," I said, "but we had to do it. He simply wouldn't listen."

"He wasn't my friend."

"Your partner, then. If he had been willing to cooperate with us we certainly would have liked to have had him on our side as well. After all, we need everyone on our side that we can get here. This is a difficult struggle and we're trying to save the world."

He stood there, pondering all of this for a while, and then said faintly, "No, I'm sorry. I just won't help you. My instructions are quite clear: to resist until the very end if captured, and I'm bound by them. Also, I think that you're lying."

"I'm not lying," I said. "Look around you. Think about the Institute. It *is* automated, you know that. I've told you the truth about this all along, and if you were only willing to release your assumptions you would know that it was the truth. Come on," I said and extended a hand toward him, gave him the smile again, "be reasonable. We can end this rotten system and have a country again in only a little while if we have the cooperation of people like you."

For a moment I thought that I might have had him then but he shook his head again and I realized that he had crossed over that delicate and perilous moment of possible submission into a position now where he could only harden. "Never," he said. "You killed Lawson. You didn't want to see if he would help or not. You just killed him. Besides, he was begging to help you."

"He was too weak," I said. "We don't need weak people. We need people with strength, true Enforcers. Your friend Lawson would never have passed the codes."

"I'm sorry," he said again, "I won't do it."

"All right," I said. There is a time to reason and a time to act. There is a time to struggle and there is a time to go with the tide. I walked past him to the flap of the tent, opening it, and peered out into the darkness where Four, as instructed, was standing duty by the fires. I gestured toward him; quickly he came to me. In many ways Four is the best of us, although he is less of a revolutionary than a servant of whoever may be leading him at a given time. "Take him," I said. "We're going to have to deprogram."

Four nodded, said nothing (he is not an articulate sort), and went into the tent, emerging an instant later with the Institute Enforcer in a pursuit grip. "I won't yield," the Enforcer said as Four dragged him along. "Everything you told me is lies. The Network is a nightmare, totally destructive and vicious. Our job is to control it. Everyone knows that that's perfectly true."

"Take him away," I said to Four, and Four took him away into the deprogramming pit, moving him right along. I followed at a cautious distance, not because my presence was necessary but because deprogramming interests me a great deal. Someday, when we have restored the land to the people, the Institute to ashes, the Network to flower, I would like to have a chance to exercise it for my own amusement.

ii

In the pit, a female is brought to the Enforcer. We keep a small stock of females in a repository near the Battery for occasions such as this and also, of course, to salve our own sexual needs. I insist upon heterosexuality in the band. Buggery and fetishism, those linked symptoms of decadence, are prevalent among the Enforcers and the residents of the Landscape; I have cultivated, at least among my little group, a fanatical attention to hetero-sexual detail. If we have sexual needs to be serviced they will be dealt with in a conventional and wholesome fashion; this is something in which I profoundly believe, and anyone in the band who is caught performing an undesireable act risks expulsion. It is for this reason that the females are kept in the repository, but they are also useful for other tasks, such as the one which I have now set before them.

In the pit the Enforcer lies, suspended underneath all of us on a bed of glass. His eyes roll doubtfully in his head, those eyes meet ours, then pass onto something above us which I cannot see but which I suspect must exist in the retrospective consciousness.

"This is not necessary," he says. "If you think that something like this can make any difference you don't know what I've done; I've—"

"No," I say, "It isn't necessary for you to speak, merely to react," and saying this I prod the female forward. She moves slowly, her limbs glazed and uneven from her long time in stasis, but as she moves toward the Enforcer her more ancient and necessary function reasserts itself and she hurls herself upon him with some simulation of real involvement. I watch them go through the motions of intercourse dispassionately as if from a great distance, at which, of course, I am since none of this has ever appealed to me particularly. Revolution is asceticism and so on and although I have never prohibited my followers from engaging in sexual activity, finding it better to cater to natural impulse than to deny it, I have not myself engaged in it for many years. There is too much other work to do: the work of the revolution, which involves overthrowing the Institutes, reestablishing our right to the land, overturning the corrupt system in which the Networks are used as elaborate detention camps for the best and most vigorous elements of society. This is what I believe; the facts of the matter have total evidency.

Meanwhile, the female is coiling and uncoiling, working over the suspended and prostrate form of the Enforcer, and finally, after a good, long time, he moans and squeals in the excess of orgasm, the jolt of it hurling the female literally from him, and he tries to reestablish connection but difficult it is, he has been so weakened and drained by the act, and therefore he merely falls with a cry into the very center of the pit and lies there for a while as the female goes away. Slowly he comes to an erect posture, then, shambling to alertness, looks at me.

"What do you want?" he says. "What do you want of me?"

"Your full cooperation," I say. "We can use you. That is why it is necessary to deprogram you."

"I don't have to be deprogrammed," he says. He looks apprehensively from Seven to Three to Eight, who are flanking me; obviously thinking that they present a rather menacing posture which, considered objectively, they probably do. Hard to detach myself and see the situation as he would. "I've told you, I've had heterosexual intercourse, I've—"

"Yes," I say, "we know all about that rape in Northerly," and he reacts with a jolt of shock, his mouth coming open stupidly. "We have a very tightly knit social system here," I say, "our own codes, our own morals, our own information network and, needless to say, our own Enforcers, and we were quite aware of what happened up there; as a matter of fact, that was one of the reasons why we found it necessary to entrap you. But of course that was merely an isolated incident," I continue as he shakes his head, runs his hands over his body in apparent disbelief. "The rape, that is to say, actually perversion, buggery, involution, all the manners and customs of the Institute are part of the very real decadence of your life. Symptoms of the decadence, I should say. What we'll have to show you is that your way of life is unhealthy whereas ours is perfectly normal."

This seems to be enough of a presentation for the moment. In any event, it is as far as I care to go at this stage. "I'll talk to you later," I say. "In the meantime I'm leaving you in my assistants' charge," and that is what I do, moving away from the spectator ring of the pit and through a side entrance. Halfway back to my quarters I am stricken by an idea, however, and instead of proceeding that way I turn around, go back to the repository in which the females are sequestered. There are twenty of them so that there is a constantly rotating stock and the monthly accident will never deter there being a sufficient quota for sexual purposes at any given time, regardless of demand.

I summon the one who has been with the Enforcer and say to her, "You are to wait one hour and return to him again."

She looks down at the ground. The females are highly submissive but this is one of the most submissive of them all, one of the reasons why she was chosen. "Do you hear me?" I say.

"Yes," she says quietly, "I hear you." There are small scars on her breasts where the Enforcer touched her. Looking at them I feel an incurious lust wedging away at me. It does not matter. "I hear you," she says again.

"The deprogramming must be complete. He must have no time whatsoever to rest."

"I understand this."

"You will have to convert him sexually within a very short and intense period of time. You were selected because I believed you equal to this, but if you have any reluctance, tell me now."

"I have no reluctance," she says. She keeps her gaze fixed on the ground. "I'll do anything that you say. We'll deprogram."

"Good," I say, "good," and turn from her, striding, loping, moving away from her at great speed, working against the choking output of twisted desire which in some way she has aroused. It must have something to do with her submissiveness. It is the nature of all the females, of course, but none more than she.

It is unfortunate but females are merely considered by us as property, and their roles are completely delimited and subservient, but on the other hand the reasons for this are quite clear and demand little explication. In the last half of the twentieth century the old sex roles were crumbling, the defined relationship of the sexes was falling apart, and this has been noted to be one of the prime causes of complete social collapse which led to the subsequent establishment of the Network/Landscape dichotomy and the perversity of the Institutes and their Enforcers. In order to command a significant revolution and to return the country to its original state it is necessary to go back to the old application of sex roles, and that is why females are treated in my unit as they are.

I understand that throughout the Network there are many other approaches to the problem and that my solution is only one of many. In some of the bands, for instance, females participate equally with males in hunting and defense activity. I do not condemn those who have chosen to perpetuate the blurring of sexual roles and identity, but I admit that I find it rather disgusting and hope that when we are able to throw the Institute over and reestablish natural, basic, contact as free men with the land, we will hold onto at least this one aspect of our present nature as I have discussed. Revolution equals asceticism equals purification. At the root, there is something disgusting about sex and them, its perpetrators.

iii

Later, when the Enforcer was brought to my quarters for the first of our long discussions, I began by pointing out to him that the use of old assassination films by the Institute was one of the prime elements of the indoctrination.

"They tried, you see, in showing you these films to build an equation between the rising tide of violence in the country and the existence of the cities. That was the point and purpose of the films but what they did not show you was this: There were cunning forces, evil men who were acting to destroy the cities. The men who set up the Institute and its programs were the same evil men who had been responsible for the subversion of the country in the first place and they continued to propound their lies through tapes and lectures which even when they, these men, were long dead would continue to be disseminated. That's the legacy that they left you."

He looked at me in a somewhat confused way, then slowly shook his head, resisting this insight. "No," he said, after staring at me in that posture of confusion for a long time, his eyes bleak and turning inward where indeed his psyche seemed to be turning, pivoting on that slow wheel of deceit which had been induced to spin within him, "that couldn't possibly be. Everything that you're saying is lies. If the Networks were to be broken, if they were to flow over the Landscape and take over our institutions, our means of protection, it would be the past all over again. The country would fall apart. You're telling me lies."

"I'm not telling you lies," I said, "you have got to see the truth; look now," and gesturing for him to follow stood and went to the open space of my quarters where

I looked out upon the Battery, through the uneven mists of the late day, looking south toward Brooklyn and in the distance the vast, unknown spaces of the sea. A little breeze came in off the Hudson, stirring the foul air of my quarters, and I said, "Can't you see? The Network has almost been cleaned again. It's no longer what they told you it was; it's been purified. That's because technology has moved out of it, because for fifty years it's been able to restore itself. If it were inherently evil the air wouldn't be clear, would it?"

He stood behind me at some distance and said, "Lies. You're telling me lies. You killed Lawson and now you're trying to kill me but I'm not afraid. I'm not afraid of any of your lies and I won't listen to anything you have to say and I'll defend the Institute as long as I can. I'm no traitor. I know what you people are."

Abruptly I lost patience. To a certain point I can be reasonable and disciplined and then, past it, some lever pushed, I become almost hysterical and lose sight of all objective reality. It is a bad trait but on the other hand I would most likely not be a leader without it; the group has a great fear of my temper and I am able to manipulate it for my own purposes. "You stupid fool," I said and charged upon him, closed that gap rapidly, and raising my left hand I hit him in the mouth.

It was like hitting paper. He gasped, knees rolled, and he fell beneath me to the floor. I forgot how gravely he had been weakened by his earlier adventures in flight, by the excesses to which we had subjected him. Still, seeing him below me, the rage did not diminish. I kicked him in a cheekbone and heard that faint grinding followed by splatter, meaning that something was broken in. "You won't listen," I said, "your Institute is run by dead men, your Institute is going to collapse of its own weight within ten years, your entire machinery is going to fall apart and leave you dead out there in the land, and meanwhile you're still being taught to fear the only people who can save you. Only the Network can save you but you won't see that," and I kicked him yet again, digging a toe into the ribs, rolling him over. "You idiot," I said, "don't you realize what a damned fool you've been, what fools all of you have been? You're merely being used, used as mercenaries to support a corrupt, evil, discredited system, but it isn't as if the system even works any more. All of the people you're supposed to be protecting are dead. Everything's dead, there's nothing out there in the land but machines and the machines are breaking down. Help us!" I shouted, and danced up and down on the ground of the enclosure in a mad little rage. "Help us! Don't you realize that we're the only people who can save you, that we are the root of your salvation?" and in order not to injure him further, render him totally useless to us (I had that much objectivity toward my own behavior), I backed away from him, toward a corner, leaving him to flounder on the floor. "Save us!" I shouted. "It's the only chance; it's the only way; we can help you, too, but we can't do it if you're going to be stupid; we need you; join us, join us!" Ancient, hallowed, revolutionary rhetoric as I understand it, to be delivered in a high, shrieking tone, but underneath all of this there was a deep well of cunning; I was contriving my effects, controlling and working them from a core of horrid objectivity as any leader must, and then I rushed toward him again, feinting yet another kick and he rolled away from me, closing his eyes, bringing his elbows up to cover them.

"Stop it!" he said, "stop it, you've got to stop it now!" I could see that I was really terrifying him now and terror is healthy, it is that good, clean purgative that can work through all of the mean levels and abcesses, leaching away the stupidity and corruption, bringing the cleansing fire, and I reached toward him then, seized him by the collar of the burlap and yanked him to his feet. His face, gleaming like a vegetable, hung in front of mine.

"You're going to help us," I said to him, "or we'll kill you. Do you want to be killed? Do you?"

I could see him calculating this, all of it working its

way through him, and then something simply broke, something within him, and the poisons began to rush out, pooling first in his eyes, which is where these things generally begin. "No!" he said, "no, I don't want to die!" and I believed him, I could sense the good, clean conviction in that voice. "I don't want to die," he said, "I don't want you to kill me; I just don't know what to believe any more, don't you understand that? I've been at the Institute all this time, they taught me one thing, they taught me to believe everything you say is lies, they threatened to throw me into the Network, that was the threat they would use if you didn't work out at the Institute because we had no other citizen's credentials and I didn't want to be in the Network, I didn't want, I didn't want—"

"But it's not so bad, is it?" I said calmly, and yanked him around again so that he could see the mists through the aperture. "It isn't what they said it was, is it? It's not such a terrible thing at all. So if they lied to you about that one thing they could have lied to you about everything else, don't you see that, don't you? Everything was lies."

He looked, stared outside, eyes bulging, and then his face came back to mine and he said, "Yes, yes, I guess that's the truth but it's too fast—"

"We have no time," I said, "no time to go slowly; your Institute is planning a massive sweep of the Network; they know, their machines know that we're on the verge of a real breakthrough and they're going to try to destroy us, they have the fire power, they just may do it . . . but it's the last thing that they'll ever do because the machines are dying. Everything is falling away; the Network will come to an end but so will your Institute. And all over the country it's happening that way, the machines are breaking down, they were all built at the same time, the programs, the lies, the dichotomy, and if we can't save ourselves now we never will. The world will end."

"All right," he said then, "all right, I don't know if

I believe you but I can't struggle anymore. I'll work with you. I'll tell you everything you want to know." Air was drained from him in a vast, gasping rush and, a dwindled, groaning parody of himself, he lowered his body to the ground, encircled knees with arms and looked up at me. "I'll tell you anything you want to know," he said. "I'll help you take the Institute back. I don't know if you're telling me the truth or not but I can't stand this anymore—"

"You believe me," I said. "I know that you believe me. It's true. Everything I've told you is true."

"I don't know," he said, "I told you, I don't know; I don't care either, it doesn't matter. But let me help you and let me bring this to an end. They did terrible things to us in the Institute; they never left us alone, they came into the corners and squeezed our lives away, our dignity; I simply don't care anymore. I'll help," he said then, "I'll help," and he extended an arm toward me in a gesture both pleading and beckoning. I could see then that what he had said was sincerely phrased and that if nothing else our relationship had entered into a new phase. I reached toward him, I seized that hand then, I helped him sobbing to his feet, I put an arm around him, I talked to him comfortingly—

—And in due course there was the sound of applause from the aperture and I turned to see that One, Two, Six, Nine, and Eleven were standing there, their hands beating like birds, their faces streaming with sweat and smiles. Approbation. I let it wash over me like the good, clean air itself while the Enforcer sagged against me in astonishment.

"They're just showing their pleasure," I pointed out to him. "There's a good deal of anxiety here and they want to help you as much as I do."

His face settled into a look of presumptive agreement and I knew then that the real deprogramming and reindoctrination could begin.

iv

So it was explained to him what he was needed to do and how he could help us and what the band would need him for. Before we went into these technicalities and details we allowed him a long, sweaty time in the repository all by himself—pick of the females, of course, and the promise of seclusion. The asceticism of the Enforcers is, as we know, quite superficial; actually they are wholly corruptible and debauched, raging with those simple desires which most of us in the Network have long ago learned to handle at the sublimative level. Still, each to his own, as they say, and it was decided that it would be best to have him working with us in a contented and cooperative frame of mind.

He therefore was given the use of the repository for a full day and night after his interview of capitulation and only then brought into my presence for an extended discussion. His appearance aroused the snickers and salacious grins of Three and Seven, his escorts, as well it might; it was a marked contrast to his earlier demeanor. In fact, he looked extremely debauched and many years older than he had looked even at the times when he was beaten. He cannot be more than twenty-one, three years and four months younger than I am, but at this moment he appeared to be in his late thirties, even early forties, the appearance, in short, of a senile, decrepit man on the verge of disaster. He was young and would bounce back, of course, but for the moment he looked quite terrible.

Staring at him, not without amusement, it occurred to me that for too many years I had overlooked the meaner delights and possibilities of the repository and that when this revolution was over, which I hoped to be quite shortly,

I would have to take advantage of sensual pleasures myself. There is no need whatsoever to maintain the habits of the revolutionary once the revolution has begun, or at least this is what I decided looking upon him.

"It was extraordinary," he said to me before I had even had a chance to make a comment. "You know, buggery is very common in the Institute; I mean, most of us were homosexuals there because there was simply no heterosexual outlet whatsoever offered, but I never felt, never felt for a minute that I was a homosexual. I knew that it was just a matter of time until I got the opportunity to prove that this was not so." He turned upon me a mysterious and ghastly smile. "The Institute misled us," he said. "You were absolutely right about that."

"Well, of course I was right about it," I said. "I'm glad to see that you've come around to seeing the truth of the matter now."

"That business in the pit," he said, still with that strange, abstracted expression, "now that was really something. I had only imagined things like that, but let me tell you, there was no need for you to use a *pit*. Why, do you know—"

"I don't know anything," I said then. "I don't want to know anything, none of that is my affair," cutting him off straightway, and then with an irritation which I was barely able to control I motioned for him to sit and told the Enforcer what we expected of him.

What we expected of him, of course, was that his knowledge of the Institute be turned to our advantage; we had maps and background but his specific knowledge of codes, access routes, pathways, various machinery, various important communication centers was invaluable, and it was also hoped, at least when we went out to capture an Enforcer, that he might even know the specific code words which would disarm the machines, open up the barriers, the Institute itself for us. It was disappointing thus to learn that the checkpoints themselves were actually manned by humans, Enforcers trained in the Institute.

We had hoped, had heard rumors that the checkpoints, too, were automated, but the knowledge that they were not, once known, could be accommodated and it was good to hear from him that the guards at the checkpoints were the least competent, the least successful of all the personnel of the Institute; they could easily be outwitted. The problems lay within the Institute itself.

"What we want to do is to seize the machinery," I said, "get hold of the computers that actually regulate and control the armaments, the tapes, the lecturers, the planning for the sweeps, the ordnance materials and so on. There must be a master computer bank somewhere, we're pretty convinced of this, and once we seize the bank the rest of it, we believe, should be quite easy. Once we have the Institute everything falls into place. We can liberate the Landscape within a matter of hours and open up the Network . . . and once we open up the Network, once we get those barriers down our problems are over."

"In other words," he said with a certain wryness, "I'm supposed to function as the point man; I'm going to be the one at the head of the column that everybody's going to be shooting at while the rest of you lay back and see if I can disarm the Institute. That's not too much of a privilege, is it?"

"On the contrary," I said, "you've got it all wrong again. You don't think that we'd go to all this trouble to capture you and deprogram you and work with you in order to take risks with your person, do you now? We intend to guard you like a rare and valuable cargo. You're essential to the success of our mission and you're going to be in the middle or rear at all times, flanked and surrounded. You're merely to pass onto us instructions as to what to do. We'll perform the necessary tasks under your instruction."

"And then, once you achieve your goal," he said, "once you get into the Institute itself then and I've helped you accomplish what you say you want, *then* you'll dispose of me. First use me and then get rid of me; isn't that the way it's all supposed to work?"

"On the contrary," I said again, "very much on the contrary; you don't really think that anybody here is in this for the power, do you? No, this is the revolution; we're talking about liberation. I'm the leader but it's a position held in trust, a temporary situation simply because at this moment in time I'm a better leader than anyone else in the band and all of us have agreed on that. Once the Institute is liberated and this miserable situation has been brought to an end, however, I see no need to continue as leader." I pointed toward him. "*You* can be the leader," I said, "it's perfectly agreeable to me, perfectly agreeable I would think to everyone, and if not my orders will hold anyway. You can take over the responsibilities, you can do anything you want. Actually," I conceded, "you understand that this phase of the revolution involves the need for strong leadership, but once the Institute is conquered and liberated all definitions of leadership itself will fall away. There will merely be individual humans living in dignity and peace with one another, no barriers between Network and the Land, no checkpoints, no armaments, each going as he pleases, living as he will, no more hostility and suspicion being bred between the two elements. So there won't be much of a cadre at all, you understand. But," I went on, "there will always have to be some administrator through whom the few basic community decisions must be funneled and you're quite welcome to that. In fact, I hope that you will take it. I'm quite tired of the ascetic, difficult life of the leader and quite frankly looking forward to leaving my responsibilities and leading a different kind of life for a while. It hasn't been easy, you know. None of this is really very easy."

He listened to this long speech solemnly and then said, "I would like to believe you. I'd like to believe that everything you say is true. But I don't trust, I'm not sure—"

"Does it seem untrue? Does anything you've learned

here go against what you've learned of the reality of the Institute?"

"No," he said. He shook his head. "That's quite true, it all makes perfect, terrible, jarring sense. But it still doesn't seem right somehow. Surely the Networks are there for a reason, and surely you can't refer to the bands as peaceable citizens who have merely been exploited, who merely want to be left alone. Not with a hard-core revolutionary such as yourself—"

"But we're all revolutionaries," I said quite openly, "of course we are. I never denied it. That's precisely the point. We live in an impossible, intolerable, inequitable situation, and at last, after all this time, it's going to be rectified. That doesn't make us evil; it just makes us perfectly reasonable. There is a lot of suffering, you know. The average lifespan in the Network is forty years. Infant mortality is up to forty percent before the seventh year, and so on. Wouldn't that make you a revolutionary?"

He spread his palms, leaned back, looking disturbingly relaxed, not at all like the disheveled, frantic youth we had brought in only a few days ago. Benefits of the repository, of course: sex as the breeder of self-confidence, superficial as that self-confidence may be.

"It might," he said. "What I want to know is this: When are we going to commence this attack upon the Institute? How long do you plan before we actually begin—"

"We're going tomorrow," I said.

And then, as his eyes dilated in astonishment, I commenced to explain.

v

So I explain to the Enforcer the reason why the attack must be made quickly and why waiting would be counterproductive, and how all along our attack has been predicated upon his cooperation, which we now have, so what is the point of waiting any longer? He seems to agree with this but I can see the doubt coruscating little pinpoints of light throughout his pupils and thus I have to devote more time to explication than perhaps is strictly necessary; I must point out to him that every day that passes the machinery of the Institute comes closer to total breakdown, that the plans being promulgated for the sweep that might kill us all grind that much closer toward possibility, that the very members of my band itself, honed to a lean and battle-bright hardness, might lose the fine edge of their training and collapse toward apathy and resentment. "You were the factor we needed," I say, "and now we have you," and the Enforcer leans back again, understanding creeping across his face, and says that he sees what I am talking about but nevertheless the imminence of the plan is a little terrifying.

Well it is, it is. I am aware of this myself and suddenly I find that the interview is beginning to circle back upon itself and is possibly self-defeating; I bring matters to a conclusion then, stating that he should leave the enclosure, take a little walk on the Battery, do anything that he needs for the next few hours for sleep and relaxation since there is nothing more to say and the morrow will bring the attack right upon us. If fortunate and on schedule, we plan to retake the Institute within a matter of hours.

"Can I go to the repository?" he says with a scatological leer, "if that will relax me?" I tell him that he can go to the repository. The resentment, bubbling cheerlessly within me, threatens to overflow when I see his stride as he leaves me.

Nevertheless, I maintain usual control as, left alone, I summon my senior aides, Five and Eight, before me, give them instructions. Quickly I give them the background of the developed situation and go on to say that I trust that they understand why the attack must begin at once, without further pause.

"I don't know," Five says, who, as I have pointed out previously, is the most submissive of the group, thus making his reaction particularly disturbing. "Why is it necessary to go so quickly? Couldn't we wait at least until we're sure that we can trust him?"

"I'm sure that we can trust him," I say. "Deprogramming has been quite effective and I see no question of its lack of efficacy at this time."

"Nevertheless," Five says—he give me a complex look composed of many factors; there is much history and apprehension intermingled in that look and momentarily I find myself disconcerted by it, shattered in fact, looking to the ground—"nevertheless, I question the haste. If an attack is efficacious now, then it will be just as efficacious in a few days. Surely we can wait until he can be trusted."

"No," Eight says. I look at him with some gratitude; it is good to hear a word of defense. "He is quite right. We will have to launch the attack immediately. After all, we have no idea how soon the sweep itself may materialize. For all we know, the fact that he and his companion are discovered missing by the Institute may accelerate the sweep. Anyway," he adds, "I can't go on living in this constant state of preparation. I think it's time for us to strike."

"Do you see?" I say to Five, considerably heartened by this line of defense. "Now you can't possibly say that there is no agreement here. This is not a unilateral decision; I'm sure that the rest of you will agree."

"Nevertheless," Five says and "neverthless," again, "I'm not sure that I like it. The conditions are not totally trustworthy."

"Still," I say, "we're going to do it. We're going to do it tomorrow," and I continue then, giving Five and Eight the highly confidential instructions as to exactly how the attack will proceed and what we have in mind and what we will do when we enter the Institute itself. Five, his old submissiveness returning—he is, if nothing else, a loyalist—listens to all of this quietly while Eight, a more thorough type, takes notes on a pad extracted from a pocket, a pencil taken from my desk, balancing them perilously on a knee. "Be of courage," I conclude, "and we cannot possibly fail."

"No," Eight says, "we will not fail."

"Pass on the word to the others," I say then and with a dismissive gesture stand. Immediately Eight stands with me but Five holds his position for several moments, precipitating a situation of vast tension. Looking at his impassive face, his strained figure, I wonder if there is, after all this time as head of the band, a confrontation ensuing but finally something within him breaks just as it broke within the Enforcer and he stands as well.

"All right," he says, "I'll go along with this. But I don't like it. I think that you're being too hasty. How do we know about the objective truth of the information he has given us? How can we be sure that he is entirely reliable? For all we know he was sent by the Institute as a plant to deliberately mislead us. They may be waiting for us. We may go directly into their line of fire."

This is certainly a disconcerting thought and one which had not previously occurred to me, but I am careful to in no way betray to Five how deeply he has shocked me. "No," I say, "that is impossible. I have checked him out deeply and his veracity is unquestioned."

"Nevertheless—"

"Nevertheless nothing," I say, "nevertheless nothing whatsoever, tomorrow we are going to strike," and saying no more I conclude the interview violently, that is to say that I gesture toward the abcess through which flow the mists of the Battery and say, "If either of you have any objection to this you're welcome to put it to a vote and to dispose of me as leader. What do I care? What do I care if the sweep comes upon us while all of us are chattering away about the line of succession?" which is cheap and in many ways an unfair trick, but then again it is important to maintain control of the situation in any circumstances and leadership itself is a brutal and forceful business. In any event it is quite enough, finally, to quiet Five; his familiar docility and terror return and he becomes gelatinous in his position, the humors of his body themselves seeming to break down to an uneven grey, and saying nothing else he and Eight leave my quarters together, Eight tugging on Five's arm and whispering something to him confidentially. I know that the two of them can be trusted, by which I mean to say that they will pass the orders to the other members of the band without question or without suggestion of opposition, which is all, truly, that I can ask at the present time, or for that matter at any time whatsoever, although it is difficult to be positive about a situation in which so much, after all, is intrinsically negative.

Alone at last in the tent I ponder my position. We will strike at dawn; we will use the Enforcer to lead us upon the Institute; with the aid of his information and his sophisticated knowledge of the Institute we will be able to penetrate the barriers. Right? Right. We may well have done better in the investment of more time in the Enforcer, quizzing him on specifics, also deep hypnotherapy and extended deprogramming might have yielded more information than he was able to consciously yield on the Institute and its devices . . . but we are pressed for time, we are extremely pressed for time, and everything considered it would be best not to waste any more of our precious chronology in our attempt to reclaim the Land.

Reclaim the Land. To reclaim the Land: This is my simple and dreadful mission. I do not know how the others may feel about this, I assume that we are drawn together by a commonality of interest and in no case have I felt impelled to draw from them, one by one, their separate reactions to the situation, but my own feelings are quite clear: There has been a massive inequity invoked and we will set it to rights. It is our obligation. More and more in recent times I have been guided by a persistent sense of outrage, a feeling that they had absolutely no right to do to us what they have done and that for reasons of simple justice, if no others, we would have to set the balance moving in the other direction. Now that has happened.

I stand there quietly in quarters for a long time, thinking about this and that and many other things, and then I decide, convulsively, that I have had enough of this, I am no less mortal and fallible than the Enforcer himself and should hie myself to the repository to partake of what I have, for so long, been denied. I am about to do this then, I am literally at the flaps of the tent, about to go there, when I realize that the Enforcer himself may be in the pit at this very time and that it would be an extremely bad breach of etiquette, I should say the perilous relationship which has been established between the two of us, to join him there. It would be an overt abandonment of my dignity. Also, I have told him already of my asceticism; it would hardly do me credit in his eyes to rupture that vow.

So I remain in the tent. But I decide, staying there, waiting for the dawn of our assault, that this will be the last time that I will deny myself and that when the revolution has been accomplished, as early as the next evening, I will permit myself the same indignities that I have so gracefully yielded to this enemy of mine. I will join the females; I will permit myself indulgences; I am entitled to everything that the rest of them are. This was the principle upon which the Institute and the Network themselves were founded, of course: one of partitions and of privilege.

Well, why not? Why not?

Now all of this will change, I think, and I stay within my tent through the fullness of the night, sleepless, girding myself against the dawn, and toward the very end (or merely, I mean, the beginning) of the night a thought extrudes itself: Am I not indulging in the same extravagances and deceit which were responsible for the establishment of the Network itself? the assignment to myself of privileges beyond my ascetic and celibate condition? I think about that and I think about other things and I consider all of the fullness of my dilemma and at last it is morning, the day of our attack against the Institute, and inside, although I have extraordinary reason to feel trepidation, all I know is the calm of the avenger . . . and that peace moves out in waves to the outer edges of myself, convincing me from top to bottom that I am ready.

vi

We moved out at dawn, then, the twelve of us plus the Enforcer. Thirteen for the attack and I refused to see any religious or mystic significance in this number, although Five brought it to my attention more than once during the ride. He did not know what to make of it.

We used two cars for the assault: a 1958 Volkswagen which had been restored to seventy-five percent of original operating efficiency through the ministrations of Nine and Four, very talented mechanical workers both of them, and the 1964 Cadillac in which the Enforcer and his companion had arrived, the car which they had wrecked due to the cunningly placed trap on which Nine and Four had similarly worked for many difficult weeks. Eight, Six, Nine, Four, and Twelve rode in the Volkswagen while the rest of us, the Enforcer and I cheek by jowl in the back, took the Cadillac, leading the Volkswagen at the instructions of the Enforcer, tracking our way up the ruined highway to the Institute.

The Cadillac was a beauty. One would have been all wrong not having had admiration for this car; the factors that had resulted in its construction might have been the same crude and abused view of reality that had led to the creation of the Network itself . . . but nevertheless, even these many, many decades later one could only appreciate the power of the car, its solidity, its weight, the way in which it responded to One's clever driving techniques which swept us clear of all interference to the east and carried us quickly, ponderously north. Easto's bands surely would have, if they had known of our plans, attached themselves in their parasitic and useless way, wanting part of the triumph without having engaged in any of the plans. I would not have shared any of it with Easto, however. After the revolution there would be enough freedom for any of us, and in the meantime, in the meantime I wanted all of the credit. This is an inevitable and human desire.

Jammed against me, the Enforcer said nothing. I could feel the weight of his buttocks; indeed I was so closely against him that I could feel the slow impact of his breath moving evenly in and out of his lungs as we staggered north, small lights from the other side of the river helping us on our way. New Jersey is another territory altogether, yet it was helping us in its own way that night. As we crossed the riverline, the first boundary, bringing us closer to the checkpoint, I felt a definite quickening and gathering in the air almost as if the air was become a blanket, bearing down upon us.

It was at this point that Five said, "Thirteen for the revolution. I don't like it."

Dawn had begun to work at the edges of the horizon, tearing back the paper of the night, and looking at the little streaks of illumination coming at us, it was easy to say to Five: "Keep quiet now."

"It isn't right," Five said again, "I'm telling you it just isn't right; it's a sign, an indication of some sort that this isn't permitted to be. We belong in the Network, they belong in the Land; it's preordained, that's what it is. I'm telling you we're going against natural law—" and overcome by a sudden feeling of revulsion I leaned forward (he was acting as point in the front) and hit him lightly, then not so lightly at all in the mouth. He sobbed and fell back against the seat. "I said it isn't right," he said again and then said nothing.

I could feel the Enforcer trembling against me. "He's right," he said.

"He's not right. He's panicking."

"No, he's not panicky," the Enforcer said, "panic has nothing to do with it. Do you think it's panic? No, it isn't; it's just the truth. We belong in the Institute, you belong in the Network. It's evil to think otherwise. I tell you we're going against natural law." His tone perfectly reproduced the accents of Five; I could understand, listening to this, the chameleonlike, fully adaptable nature of the Enforcers that enables them to blend so well with the very Network that they are committed to destroy. "Anyway," he said, "even if it isn't natural law it's crazy. We'll never get through. Never get through checkpoint; they'll shoot us down in place. Do you think that the barriers are stupid? I'm telling you, they know what the hell they're doing."

"Enough," I said. Something dramatic was necessary on the moment or the entire attack would collapse under the weight of its implication. Behind us, turning, I could see the Volkswagen probing its way through the dawn fog, slowly keeping pace in the darkness, forms jammed within. Twelve, driving, would know enough to stop. "Stop," I said to One. "Stop!" and he obeyed me instantly, the power-drum brakes yanking us to a halt, and even before the car had stopped fully I had taken out my pistol and leveled it at Five, who gave me a most astonished, furtive expression. Behind us I could hear the drone of the Volkswagen as it braked.

"Enough," I said, "get out."

"No," Five said, "you can't—"

"I won't tolerate it," I said. "You're fucking up everything, all of our careful plans. I won't have you panicking. Get out and make your own way south."

"They'll kill me," Five said. "Northing's bands are all over here, I don't have a chance." He motioned to the W on his clothing; we were going in full battle insignia, of course, as befitted an expedition of this nature. "I'll keep quiet," he promised, "just give me another chance."

"No chance," I said, "no chance," and raising the pistol, drilled him neatly through the skull. Already he had been launched in the process of leaving the car; his form spun against the door, the door sprung open, he fell into the mud, carried by the momentum of his own desire as well as death. One at the wheel sighed. Otherwise it was very quiet. I leaned over and pulled the door closed. "Let's get going," I said, "let's get out of here."

One put his foot to the accelerator, the Cadillac moved out. The Volkswagen's lights continued to probe at us, following, as if nothing whatsoever had happened. I put the pistol away inside my clothing, turned to the Enforcer. "It was quite necessary," I said.

"I know. I had to do the same thing with Lawson."

"Your friend. The one you came in with."

"Yes," he said. His face was solemn. "He was panicking, too. Really, it's the same situation, isn't it? The same thing. You and I, we're up against exactly the same things. I was trying to get into the Network, you're trying to make it into the Institute. Panic. We have to deal with panic."

"Yes," I said. If it made the Enforcer feel any easier to make this equation between the two of us I would hardly have had the temerity to oppose him. My mind was abstracted, stumbling away toward other issues.

"Weakness," he said. "Every time you want to get something done you have to fight the people who don't want to have a thing changed. It's difficult, isn't it? It's difficult," and gave me that ingratiating smile again; I gave it back to him, it was all the same to me. Anything to make the Enforcer happy. I was glad to have done what I did with Five; he was too soft, essentially, to participate in the revolution anyway, but murder is always shocking, no matter against whom it is committed. I closed my eyes, leaned back into the seat, listened to the whine of the motor. One propelled the car steadily through the fog. "It really is an awfully good thing that we're doing this now, aren't you ready to say that?" the Enforcer asked. "I mean, if the Institute is as near to failure as you say it is, if the whole system is going to collapse, then you can really say that what we're doing is saving people. We're saving the system itself from its own collapse. Wouldn't you agree with that?"

"Whatever you say," I said, "whatever you say," and kept my eyes closed then, shut him out, withdrew my hip from his and lay back in the seat, letting the small and familiar images play themselves against the screen of my mind, working neither for nor against them, hearing the sounds of the motor, hearing the dark sound of the Volkswagen behind us, trying to clear out for myself some abcess of space and silence in which I would be able to continue with those small and necessary acts which would make all things possible . . . but not enough time, never enough time, never enough time at all; in less time than I would have calculated we were hard up against the checkpoint itself and the true testing to begin. I heard One's intake of breath as the car was braked; I felt the Enforcer scrambling against me; I inhaled and smelled the odors of Five's blood . . . and then the car bucked to a halt and I knew that what would happen next would happen very quickly and I only hoped that the work I had done in preparation for this would be sufficient. But who is to know? Who is to know of any of this; who is to really know? And then what began to happen took place very quickly and there was nothing to do but to go along with it.

Even leaders, *mostly* leaders, are swept up by the tide of events, I think. This is an aphorism.

vii

Quickly we shoot the guard at the checkpoint. It is One who does it with a rolling shot from the gun held near his armpit, the guard falling, little streams of blood yanked from his forehead along with a single scream and then, from the woods behind him, another guard leaps, back-up force no doubt, a long rifle extended toward us like an erect cock. I think about this for a moment, the amusing correlation between weapons and male sexual apparatus, but not in any way which distracts me from disposing of this second guard with a deadly shot into the duodenum; he opens like a bag of blood and from him pours a clear, gelatinous stream of fluid, arcing in the air, then One hits the accelerator, screaming, and we are through. All around us my troops are bellowing in delight, first blooding, the confrontation never worse in the real than it was in the imagination and I permit them their brief elation, although it is the Enforcer who concerns me. He has not moved since the first shot was fired. The Volkswagen holds steadily on course behind us, straight up the hill, and for the first time now the Institute is in sight, reaching up before us. The Enforcer is pale. His eyes are closed, his respiration shallow. I tap him in the stomach.

"Don't panic now," I say. "Remember, you were the one who talked about panic. Here we are. We broke through the barrier without serious resistance. I told you they didn't know what they were doing any more."

"You killed them," he says, "you killed both of them. You killed Institute personnel, you killed guards."

"Of course we did. We had to."

"Are you afraid of killing?" One asks in violation of the specific instructions I had given before the journey that all conversations with the Enforcer were to be conducted only through me. Remembering this, he hunches over the wheel but it is already too late; the Enforcer has heard One.

"No," he says, "I'm not afraid of killing. Killing's all right; we killed plenty of people to get down there, we're trained to kill people. But what if you're wrong? What if you've lied to me?"

"I haven't lied to you."

"What if you haven't lied to me but we're killed at the Institute, all of us? What if you're killed and I'm captured? I'm a turncoat, an infidel. They'll torture me to death."

"No, they won't," I say. "They won't do that." It is preposterous that I should be spending these vital moments in soothing the Enforcer but he is vital. "We can't possibly lose," I say, "there's no chance of defeat whatsoever. Look how easily we got through the barrier. It's almost over now."

"Still," he says, "still—" and at that moment we are thunderstruck by a booming explosion. We come to a crashing halt and I can feel the outlines of rock literally poking up through the seat. One is screaming and twisting the wheel and then we are alone on the empty road below the Institute, the Institute looming up above us.

One says, "We've got to get out! We've got to get out!"

"Yes," I say, "yes," knowing that the situation is serious. Quickly I shout desperate orders to the others in the car but they have already heard, are springing out the door for their lives, the Enforcer first of all, hitting the grass, the sun now up fully around us, a brilliant yellow amid the green foliage. I hit the grass hard, feel my mouth going into the black, bitter soil, and then roll, my first sight that of the Volkswagen, which seems to have taken a similar jolt to its underside, rolling to a halt; Twelve, the driver, already in midair, springing for freedom, and I watch this with one part of my consciousness while with the other, still trying to evaluate what has happened to us,

I look far up the hill where I see an automatic tracking device of some sort, a howitzer or antique cannon leveling in. Monitor, radar, sensors. They have located us not through cunning, but rote. I can hear the sound of a new shell being cranked into the device.

"Watch it!" I scream unnecessarily, because already my band has scattered before the impact. The screaming shell passes over all of us and hits the Volkswagen dead center. The car, down at the edge of the hill, shatters like a smashed egg, bursts into terrible flame, rolls off the road and into the gully below.

"Now!" I shout, "move!" calling to my troops, rising to my feet, dragging the Enforcer into a standing position, and then, kicking him violently to keep him moving, to keep him in view at all times, I begin to race up the hill toward the Institute, screaming. The cannon wheels stupidly toward the sound of the screaming but I put it out of commission with a grenade.

And then as we pass a rise the full splendor of the Institute is revealed to us. The low square buildings are lined against one another. The concrete and glass surfaces twinkle. The strange grassy lanes gape emptily at us.

"The machinery!" I shout to the Enforcer, "Where is the machinery?" And he babbles madly, gesticulates, dances, shakes. I kick him in the buttocks and he turns toward me, his eyes moistening to pain and knowledge. "I want the machinery, you fool!" I say. "Do you think that I went through all of this not to hear from you now?" and shaking, moaning, he points in a direction toward the east. I gesture toward the band then and we begin a wild, loping run in the direction toward which the Enforcer has pointed. Metal whizzes around us, a dull rumble, a feeling of heat underneath; the Institute in its clumsy way is trying to retaliate but too late, too late; the machines, exactly as I thought, are dilapidated, the sensor devices virtually demolished, and there is little that the blind machinery of the Institute can do except to shoot pellets harmlessly between us. There is a shriek behind; turning, I see Seven fall, hit, clutching his chest. So this proves that the Institute is not so helpless after all, if only blindly they have inflicted one casualty. But one casualty is not so bad; if it can be held to that level we have taken virtually no serious opposition whatsoever, and so I follow the Enforcer, who has moved out to the front of us into the bowels of a building. Apparently he has decided that his future, if any, lies with us; no twisted loyalties now, he has committed himself to us totally. I follow his form without thinking further, flailing away with my pistol in the air to discourage any potential assassins who might want to take a chance, but I do not think, waving, that there is any serious opposition whatsoever. We are in a dull, cool place surrounded by whir and I realize that we have come to the nest of the engines themselves.

viii

The rest is simple, almost routine. We disarm the machines, yanking out their leads and sockets, we scatter through the Institute with weaponry looking for any pockets of resistance. The Enforcer leads us to the public address system.

I make a brief statement of liberation to the students of the Institute, informing them of what has been done and why, and what the course of their lives for the next few days will be under martial law, until we begin to bring the situation to hand.

The students actually applaud this announcement, but then, as I expected from the Enforcer, there is little revulsion in the Institute against its demolition; they are a sullen group indeed who are there against their will, and liberation can represent to them only a physical fact of prolonging their fate. It is all quite simply accomplished.

There is, of course, no one in the Institute other than students, I had not expected there to be, and not two hours after the assault, I am sitting in the proctor's office, the situation totally under control, drinking some refreshing, reconstituted fructose from the commissary shelves and contemplating assignments to the members of my band during this brief transition period.

Seven, of course, will have to be buried with honors and I order Twelve and Ten, efficient mechanics both of them, to work out something for an interment and gravesite, while Two, who is quite articulate, works on a speech of some sort which will sum up Seven's life. Truly he died gloriously. To Nine I give the difficult task of the actual day-by-day administration of the Institute, supplying the students' needs, indocrinating them, and so on, and to

Six I give the job of researching the actual program through which we will make contact with other Institutes as well as the bands to the South of us in order to spread the glad news of liberation.

I sit there alone in the administrative office until the Enforcer enters. He has regarded me throughout these last moments with a mixture of awe and humility so profound that if I were not a dedicated revolutionary I would probably find it unsettling. As it is his response means little to me whatsoever. I direct him to bolt the door and then I lean back upon the gigantic chair of the Administrator (who must have died a long, long time ago), relaxing for the first time, and look upon him calmly, dispassionately, measuring him.

"Now what?" he says after I have shown no disposition to speak. "What are you going to do with me?"

"Do with you?" I say. "Why should we do anything with you? We owe you everything. You enabled us to take the Institute."

"I enabled you to do nothing. You know that perfectly well; you could have done all of it yourself." He looks down at the floor as if what he says next chagrins him which, I am sure, it does. "You were quite right," he says. "The Institute was about to fall. We offered you no resistance whatsoever."

"We?"

"Well," he says with that abashed grin again, "well then, *they*. I must feel some emotional connection to the Institute, after all. I mean, a week ago I was part of it."

"You're still part of it," I say, "you'll always be part of it."

"But not quite that way," he says, "not the way I was."

"True," I say, "that's quite true, but life is flux, as you know, and you will have to adapt. No, we're not going to kill you. We mean you no harm whatsoever; as I say, you are responsible for our victory and if we could have done it without you, well, without you, we might never have tried. You gave us the necessary confidence. The point is, the point is now that we have the Institute the true work is only beginning. We can begin to free the Network stage by stage, bit by bit, but the work is long and difficult. We will need someone to go out among the bands in certain sections to tell them that they have been liberated. Nine is a good information officer but he can only reach those bands within range of communications devices. Many in the Network live in total isolation."

"Are you asking me to do that?" the Enforcer says. "Is that your idea? Carry the news of liberation through all of the bands?"

"Something like that."

"They'll kill me," he says. "They'll kill me on sight."

"Not necessarily," I say. "They've been waiting for the news of liberation for a long, long time and you'll be briefed on exactly what you should say in order to appear as one of them. Don't worry about that. The question is, do you want to do it?"

The Enforcer stares at me stupidly with that same bland directness I have noted a few times before in my enclosure. "I'd like some females," he says.

"The females are coming. They are on their way. The repository is the first to partake of liberation, and besides my troops are expecting it. They'll be here by nightfall. I've detailed cars from the Institute pool already."

"Then I guess I have nothing else to request," the Enforcer says. "If you want me to spread the news of liberation I will. After I have a chance with the females. If you'll permit me, of course."

"Oh, we'll permit you anything," I say, "and we'll give you a full indoctrination so you have nothing to be concerned about. You're a fast learner," I say. "I compliment you."

"Well, thank you," he says, "thank you very—"

"I think I'd prefer to be alone now," I say, standing. "So unless you have anything else to say—"

"Oh no," he says, "oh no." He comes to his feet, his posture awkward, the easy assurance of a moment ago wiped clear of his face. It is as if at the moment the relationship between us is reestablished, his fear is reconstituted. Good. This is an excellent sign, I think, following him toward the door. "Nothing at all," he says and turns toward the door, goes toward the door, opens the door then and moves halfway out.

I carefully remove my Smith and Wesson point thirty-two caliber from its genuine leather shoulder harness and shoot him in the base of his skull. He falls heavily in the door frame, half in, half out, and lies there, his head blown away. I put the pistol back in its rig and turn him over. He has died content, I'm sure. He died in optimism and fullness. Nothing was taken away from him at all.

He was certainly left a better and happier person than the one we found.

I use the intercommunications device, a fascinating mechanism, to summon Three who I have left on post and ask Three to take the corpse away. He complies quickly, saying nothing to me, putting his arms under shoulders for an easy half drag, half carry. There is nothing, after all, to say. Three knows the situation as well as I do. After he is gone I close the door and I sit in the cool isolation of the office, enjoying for the first time the genuine privacy, the real benefits of my position. It has been a long time since I have felt both so protected and so much at peace.

ix

So I go to a projection room and have Two and Seven, who have returned from their duties, set up some films for me. From the stolen instructional materials, plus what I have been able to tell them about the nature of the projector, they are able to work quickly and efficiently.

When they are done, Seven asks: "Can we stay?"

"Certainly not," I reply.

And without a word of protest they go. I find the lock for the door on a control panel in the seat which I occupy, the master viewing seat, and with another switch I darken down all the lights and then I run the film. The devices of the Institute are marvelous. It is a pity that they have become so decrepit but, of course, the essential materials are there and they will be able to repair them under my direction.

I decide to watch Zapruder, that fascinating film about which I have heard so much but have not, until this moment, had the actual opportunity to witness. It turns out to fulfill all of my expectations. Over and over again I watch Kennedy's brains pulped into crimson flowers; over and again, forward and reverse, I watch the reactions of the spectators, of the wife bolting toward the door, of the guarding forces, of the Vice-president, of the other cars in the motorcade. It is a perfect microcosm of so many forces which were at that time coming to focus in the country and it is a pleasure for once to see something live up to its billing; Zapruder is everything that they said it was.

I can barely relinquish it, so delightful and informative do I find it, so rich and iridescent in all of its colors, but after a while, reluctantly, I turn away and insert another reel, one left me by the ever-alert Two.

In this one I watch the activities of the subsequent Kennedy on the evening of his own slaughter. Kennedy the younger dies sensationally. No one could have loved death more or submitted to it with more grace than this small, vigorous man. Surely he had glimpsed death in all of its phases, run it over and over again in his mind on a hundred terrified nights, the terror leading finally to numbness, in order to allow death to take him with such grace. In those inert eyes, staring fishlike from the floor, there is perfect comprehension, this is what I was waiting for, those eyes are saying, this is what I truly wanted . . . and I feel a sense of reverence for a man, any man who can manage to gain through such sacrifice and pain his heart's desire. Sitting in the darkened screening room, I literally sob with delight; in many ways I have always identified with Kennedy the younger and he is everything that I had thought him to be.

This takes a considerable amount of time to run through and there is only time then for a brief skim-through of highlights of other films: I watch a few riots and I watch some violent deaths, people leaping off burning buildings, people immolating themselves in flaming gasoline, but after the grand and flawless beauty of the Kennedys I find these unsatisfying, and so I allow the films to drone to whiteness, the film slapping against the projector flickering darkness on the harsh light on the screen. My own fingers drum against the arms of the chair as I think about where I have been and where I am now and where I am going.

I am going to go on in the direction already well-launched, that much is clear, but to say that is not to say enough. It is a long way from Southway's ravages to the leadership of the toughest band in Westerly to this screening room in the Institute itself, but the Institute is only the beginning and were I to stop now it would be, of course, as if everything I had done was pointless, because unless my position is buttressed, the Institute almost certainly will fall and quickly. These people are no fools. Reports of the difficulty will almost certainly have reached them already and, as clumsy as is their technology, as rigid as are their bureaucratic devices, they will try to move in and wipe out this spot of infestation as quickly as they can. Perhaps two weeks. Long enough to make preparations, but not very long at all if I am to hold the position.

I will do so. My momentary stasis passes and realizing how much lies before me and what must be done in order to consolidate the small gains that I have already made, much less to fulfill my ambitions, I am filled with terror. I put on all of the lights, use the intercommunications device, summon all of the members of my band and arrange to meet them in the assembly hall in five minutes. It will be a good enough occasion to say a few words in memory of Seven, who I am informed is ready for interment, and it will also be the right and proper time to tell them that our true work is only beginning.

If you would like a complete list of Arrow books please send a postcard to P.O. Box 29, Douglas, Isle of Man, Great Britain.

Other Arrow Books of interest:

ELRIC OF MELNIBONÉ

Michael Moorcock

Melniboné: no longer the mighty empire that once dominated the world but a waning kingdom, dependent on trade from the human nations which have begun to challenge its power.

On the Ruby Throne sits Elric, the albino – sorcerer and warrior. A melancholy philosopher at odds with his destiny. As fleets of marauders probe the defences of the Dragon Isle, Elric faces treachery within his own court – from Yrkoon, the cruel and ambitious cousin who dreams of usurping him . . .

80p

Bestselling science fiction from Arrow

All the books listed below are available from your bookshop or newsagent or you can order them direct. Just tick the titles you require and complete the form below.

☐	2001: A SPACE ODYSSEY	Arthur C. Clarke	95p
☐	THE NIGHT SHAPES	James Blish	80p
☐	A CASE OF CONSCIENCE	James Blish	85p
☐	THE JAGGED ORBIT	John Brunner	£1·75
☐	STAND ON ZANZIBAR	John Brunner	£1·50
☐	THE SODOM & GOMORRAH BUSINESS	Barry Malzberg	85p
☐	RITUALS OF INFINITY	Michael Moorcock	80p
☐	ELRIC OF MELNIBONÉ	Michael Moorcock	80p
☐	ELOISE	E. C. Tubb	80p
☐	THE HERITAGE OF HASTUR	Marion Zimmer Bradley	£1·25
		Postage	
		Total	

ARROW BOOKS, BOOKSERVICE BY POST, PO BOX 29, DOUGLAS, ISLE OF MAN, BRITISH ISLES

Please enclose a cheque or postal order made out to Arrow Books Limited for the amount due including 8p per book for postage and packing for orders within the UK and 10p for overseas orders.

Please print clearly

NAME ....

ADDRESS ....

....

Whilst every effort is made to keep prices down and to keep popular books in print, Arrow Books cannot guarantee that prices will be the same as those advertised here or that the books will be available.